Her Cowboy's Way

Starla Kaye

ISBN

Her Cowboy's Way Copyright 2015 Starla Kaye
Cover Copyright 2015 R. J. Savage

Published 2015
Printed by Black Velvet Seductions Publishing
A division of Savage Publications

Visit us at:
www.blackvelvetseductions.com

Chapter One
The Bride Wore Red

Brandi couldn't go through with this. Panic chased rational thought away. Her mind swirled with visions of Runaway Bride, with her in Julia Roberts' role as the bride. She was supposed to be a June bride.

A wedding meant all kinds of serious stuff. It wouldn't be all about her anymore. Instead of stretching over the entire bed at night she would share it with Colby, fight with him for covers or about not wanting them. She would be expected to act civil in the morning before she jump-started her brain with half a pot of coffee. He had a disgusting habit of rising and shining as soon as his feet hit the floor. There would be all sorts of compromising on furnishing their home. Typical bachelor, he was almost minimalistic; she was more the eclectic type with lots of knickknacks around. Not that she had much of her own yet, but her father was letting her mother's collections go to her new home. Colby had agreed, but she saw the way he'd ground his teeth in frustration when her father made the offer.

Then there was Colby's attitude about expecting obedience, at least on issues he believed strongly about. Following what someone else wanted of her had never been her best trait.

She glanced at the expensive wedding gown hanging in the room used for brides in the church in which she'd grown up. Obedience. Love, honor and obey. Did she really have a grasp on what the word meant? Not according to her father. Not according to most people in town. She tended to go her own way about things…and sometimes paid a price for it. Considering Colby had known her most of her life, he understood that she had trouble staying within boundaries.

Boundaries, she saw them as "guidelines" or "lines drawn in the sand." To her they were things that could be seen as a bit flexible or moved an inch or two or several feet. He'd heard her complain numerous times about having gotten her bottom burned because she misinterpreted a guideline or overstepped a line seen differently by someone else—usually her father.

She wasn't sure why all of a sudden she'd become obsessed with the three key words in the wedding ceremony. Maybe because they were big words—okay, small letter-wise—but huge in meaning.

Last night at the dress rehearsal, she'd been too lost in the excitement of the moment to think about the vows and what she'd be promising. She hadn't even thought about them when Colby had teased her as he'd dropped her off at her father's ranch. But now she recalled seeing the hint of challenge in his dark eyes as he'd taunted her with "love, honor and obey."

Had he been referring to a few weeks ago when she'd told him she wanted to cut off her almost waist-length hair and dye it auburn? She wanted a change; something she'd thought would make her look more mature. His immediate response: "Absolutely not!" Which rubbed her wrong, made it a dare. Of course, she'd done both. Yet, with the first cut of her long locks, she'd about had heart failure. There wasn't any going back at that point. At least she'd managed not to whimper through the rest of the haircut and as the beautician colored her hair from blonde to red. She gaped in the mirror afterward, shocked at the drastic change, somewhat traumatized, and hated what she'd had done.

She blew out a frustrated breath. Colby hadn't taken her decision well. Disgust played a big part in his reaction, although he'd shown some sympathy when she shed a few tears about the shorter hair. After she calmed down, grumbled about regretting her impulsive rebellion, he'd turned her bottom red. If she had just listened to what he said… If she wouldn't get her back up… Yada, yada, yada.

The truth was that she'd been born breach, couldn't even manage to "obey" (follow, really) the normal way of being born. And she'd spent twenty-six years disobeying her father's rules whenever she pleased and then suffering the consequences, which never pleased her. Marriages were about equal partnerships, not having to follow anyone's rules. They were about adult relationships, about sex. She was okay with the "sex" thing. Especially with Colby.

At the thought of the six-foot-three, sinfully handsome cowboy, delicious warmth curled inside her. They'd lived on neighboring ranches since her family had moved here to Hinkley, Kansas, when she was eight. As a foolish teenager, she'd had a crush on him, which hadn't gone well. He'd been such a jerk when he'd discouraged her advances. While away at college, she'd dated a lot and explored her passionate nature. In spite of his "jerk" title, no guy had ever compared to Colby. In her fantasies, she put him on some kind of super guy pedestal, had given him impossible skills: expert at kissing, expert in all possible ways of making love. The list went on and on.

She trembled at the memory and what she'd learned were his real skills in these last six months.

Looking out over the town from her window seat, she thought about how she'd come back to Hinkley after graduation from college and getting her masters. Her original plan was to open a one-person accounting firm with only the guarantee of her father as a client. Now she had several ranchers as clients, including Colby. Their client-accountant relationship had gone many steps further, steps that had led to her bed, to his bed, and soon to their bed. What that man could do in between the sheets or on top of them. She moaned. Oh yeah, what he could do!

"Time to get dressed," Sarah announced, as she all but bounced into the room, shoulder-length brown hair fluttering around her. Her best friend since childhood looked at the white dress with layers of satin and lace. She sighed in the same way she did every time she saw the gown. "You're going to look like a princess."

Brandi hadn't picked out the dress; her father had. He'd always called her "his little princess"—except when she was in trouble—and he wanted her to look like royalty on her wedding day. Colby hadn't seen the gown yet, but he'd like it, too. You couldn't get more feminine than in this dress. He was all about feminine, all about her being a lady. Okay, he wanted her to behave like a lady. Behave! Obey. She had to admit that she had problems with both words and their definitions. The dictionary needed to be updated to include her interpretations of the definitions: follow societal or other's rules if you so choose.

She looked at her friend, who rarely strayed into the "gray areas" and accepted the common definitions of those bothersome words. Maybe Colby should marry a woman like Sarah, someone who would never challenge him or give him grief. Still, she'd have to shake him if he chose to marry someone else.

"I think this might be a bad idea," she said in growing distress. She was too young to be tied down to one man. Right? She was just starting to grow into the role of being an adult and being responsible. Okay, she was scared clear down to her bones. What if she screwed up Colby's life? He needed a good woman at his side, one who…wasn't her.

Sarah was reaching to take the dress down and glanced in her direction, her brow furrowed. "Bad idea? What are you talking about?"

Perched on the window seat overlooking the parking lot where guests were already arriving, Brandi pulled her legs up and hugged her knees. Still wearing jeans, she rested her chin on the comforting denim. "This whole marriage business. I'm not sure if it's really my kind of thing."

Sarah's eyes widened. "You're kidding, right? You're about to wear this stunning gown, walk down an aisle lined with gorgeous white roses, and take the hand of THE studliest man on earth in marriage. It doesn't get any better than that." She looked at Brandi as if she were an alien who'd taken over her best friend's body. "Oh, don't tell Thad what I said about Colby. Thad's studly, too. Just in a different way."

Brandi couldn't deny that Colby Pennington was "studly," a lot of the women in town called him Super Stud Cowboy behind his back. Yes, she'd started it off and, yes, he knew about it and that she'd been behind the nickname. Disgruntled, he'd warmed her bottom when he'd found out, which still irritated her. You'd have thought he'd been proud of the nickname! Jeez.

"No, I won't say anything to Thad." He was okay looking, but hardly "studly."

Putting aside all of those thoughts, Brandi looked at the gown. She didn't care about the dress or the roses. She wasn't that much of a flower person. But Sarah's mention of Colby's hand had brought back to mind that whole behaving matter, the whole obedience issue she'd been mulling over the last few minutes. She'd experienced a number of spankings from the man who'd been her lover for the last couple of months and who'd tolerated her as his best friend's kid sister for years.

Beyond that, she'd also already had a number of lectures from him on professional behavior, claiming he wanted to help her. Her work schedule, in particular, was an issue. If she wanted to keep sporadic work hours, come and go as she pleased, it was her business, she'd told him. He'd pointed out that building a reputation was important, which meant showing her clients she could be counted on for her skills and for being available on a regular basis. Okay, she'd eventually agreed with him. And her clients had appreciated her adjusting to normal office hours.

Then there had been a discussion about her inappropriate dress for the office. Again, her office. Again, she'd stopped wearing jeans to work and switched to dresses or suits. Most of the time. And, again, her clients had noticed the change, commented on it in approval. Did he have to be right about every little thing?

In his series of lectures on behavior—as she referred to the discussions in private, he'd gone on to mention that he expected to be the head of their household. He hadn't gone into specifics and she hadn't asked. Blind lust had kept her thoughts focused on more interesting areas. But now she was having a serious back-to-reality moment.

She faced Sarah, nerves twisting within her. "I need to talk to Colby." Alarm seemed to be taking over her mind. "Now. Right now."

Sarah blinked in horror. "You can't see him until the ceremony! It's bad luck." She shook her head. "No. No, no, no. Absolutely not."

Brandi wasn't a superstitious person, but she knew what she needed. She needed to see Colby. Panic rose to another level and her voice was harsher than she intended when she said, "There won't be a ceremony unless I talk to Colby." She pointed to the door Sarah had closed on entering. "Please. Just go get him."

"But—"

Brandi raised her chin, surprised when she battled tears. "Get Colby."

Colby struggled with his tie while his long-time friends stood around him, harassing him about getting married. He was about to give up on the tie and toss it in the trash when Sarah raced into the groom's dressing room. Brandi's best friend's face flamed in embarrassment as her gaze darted around taking in her surprised fiancé, Thad, Brandi's father, and the other two men. It was plain she would rather be anywhere else but here. He had a bad feeling about this.

"What's up?" Colby asked when she hadn't spotted him in the far corner. His bride-to-be was up to something. Hell, she was always up to something. She would be a trial in his life for the next fifty or so years, but he felt damn lucky about that. He didn't mind her going nose-to-nose on things with him every now and then; it kept their relationship interesting. He couldn't marry a woman who "Yes'd" him all the time, kind of like Sarah did Thad. He liked a woman with guts…most of the time, anyway. 'Course when she decided to cut all that long, silky hair off… Well, he hadn't liked that so damn much.

Still, as troublesome as she could be at times, he loved Brandi clear to his long, skinny toes. For every irritating trait she had, there were more that pleased him. She could be grumpy first thing in the morning, but he could live with that. She had a tendency to be far too casual with her professional appearance and with her work habits, but she'd been working on that. She struggled making the change from college kid to businesswoman. They'd already talked about this matter and she listened to him, for the most part. He would keep helping guide her since he had more real world experience.

As her husband, he intended to help guide her at home, too. He'd explained his role in their marriage, heading their household, as a good, loving man should, in his opinion. She'd been hesitant about the matter, particularly when he'd said there might be times when his "guidance" would involve taking her over his knee. The idea of continuing to get her bottom warmed as a married woman hadn't set right with her, at first. After a fair amount of lovemaking that night, pleasing her in every way she desired, she'd decided he could play whatever role he wanted. She trusted him and that meant a whole lot to him. He wouldn't ever abuse her trust. He loved and respected her.

Sarah looked uncertain, standing there in her hot pink gown. He put aside his musings. "What's the problem?"

She had trouble meeting his eyes. "Brandi said she needed to talk to you."

"She can't talk to him now," Sam Dalton protested, striding over, his forehead pinched in irritation.

Sarah worried her lower lip and focused on Colby. "She said something about there not being a ceremony unless she talks to you. Please. Come talk to her."

Colby let the ends of the bowtie dangle and nodded. "I'd best go have a few words with her then."

Her father, his folks, dang near half the town had worked hard to pull this fancy wedding together. He and Brandi would have been happy enough with just a couple of people to stand up with them to get married. But, as his mother made it clear to him, weddings were for everyone else, not so much the bride and groom. He didn't plan on disappointing any of them today. Brandi wouldn't want to either. This was just some kind of "cold feet" thing, he was sure of it. She needed settling. She needed his help, a reassurance of his love and his being there for her.

He walked over to Sarah, tried to give her a calming look. She still appeared concerned. But she tended to be a fretter. He glanced back at the frowning men behind him. "This is just a minor delay. I'll take care of things."

Colby trailed after a distressed Sarah toward the bride's dressing room. Poor Sarah, she was a nervous wreck. There wasn't a superstition she didn't know about, didn't worry about. This whole business of him—the groom—seeing the bride before the ceremony was driving her crazy. Sarah grumbled unhappily with each step back through the church. She stopped at the end of the hallway. "Last minute nerves. That's all." She sounded like she wanted his reassurance again.

"I'm sure it is. Everything will be fine, you'll see," he said and gave her a smile. It might take a few minutes of unpleasantness, but he'd get the wedding back on track. He knew in his heart that Brandi was depending on him to do so.

When they grew closer, he found the door to the bride's room was shut and Brandi's two bridesmaids stood in the hallway, annoyed. One of them turned on Sarah as she walked up. "She won't let us into the room. She demanded to be left alone. What's going on? We should be helping her get dressed. Doing something with her hair."

"Ummm…" Sarah glanced at Colby, desperate for his help.

"My bride-to-be appears to be panicking." He gave the women his most reassuring smile. "Getting married is stressful."

They still looked concerned. Time was drawing close. It worried him a bit, too. He moved in front of the door. "Why don't you ladies go make sure everything in the sanctuary looks all right? Give Brandi and me say… twenty minutes."

For a second they didn't move, and then Sarah took charge. "You heard the man. He wants some time alone with Brandi." She took off briskly in the other direction and the doubting pair followed her.

Time to face your nervous bride. He sucked in a steadying breath and knocked on the door. "Brandi Lynn."

There wasn't much time for handling this matter. Guests were already filing into their seats. The organist was already playing. And, no doubt, Sam Dalton was having trouble controlling his desire to come handle whatever the problem was in the firmest, most fatherly manner.

A way that would no doubt involve applying his hand to his daughter's bottom. But his time of punishing her was in the past. As of today—well, even before today, spanking her when needed was Colby's duty.

As the lock clicked open, he steeled himself not to lose his temper because he'd grown anxious about the necessity to get ready for the ceremony, too. This was essential. Brandi was important.

"I'm not agreeing to obey you in the vows. It's a deal breaker," Brandi said in a rush as Colby walked into the room. She looked so small, so on the edge. Her eyes were big, glistening with unshed tears. At that moment, she appeared every bit of the ten years younger than him. Not child-like, just younger and less experienced. Yet he saw the need for him to pull her through this bout of nerves.

He calmly closed and locked the door behind him. He didn't say a word, trying to determine how to handle this. He didn't want to scare her even more, he needed to bolster her confidence that this was her decision, not something he was forcing on her. She'd been standing close to the door, now she stepped backward. And, backward some more.

He moved toward her, calm, collected, determined. "A deal breaker, huh?"

She looked frustrated, a pinch of worry between her eyebrows. "This is fundamental, Colby! I'm fine with the whole love and honor stuff."

Good to hear. "But the word obey bothers you." It wasn't like he wanted her to do everything he said and not have a mind of her own. He wasn't always right. What he wanted, expected, was for her to give credence to his telling her not to do something, which would only be said for her own good. "Maybe you should explain your thinking on the matter."

She put a hand on her stomach, a sign she was jittery. "I've spent my life obeying and following rules. I'm ready to be in charge of my own life. For Pete's sake, Colby, I have my own business."

In truth, she'd always struggled with doing what someone else wanted. As for rules, she preferred to make her own or bend someone else's to meet what she wanted. He was going to have his patience tried for years to come. He decided it might be wise to respond with care. "Yes, you do. And I'm proud of what you've accomplished."

Some of the tension eased from her shoulders. "Thank you." She nibbled on her lip, still concerned.

He wasn't sure quite what she wanted yet. "You are in charge of your life. Our getting married doesn't change that."

"But… You have rules. You have expectations of me." She inched backward again.

Colby glanced at his watch. Time was not their friend. This wasn't a serious problem; she was grasping at straws, at anything, in her anxious-bride worry. "Do you love me, Brandi? Really love me?"

He stepped in front of her as cautiously as when he approached a frightened horse. Her eyes widened at his closeness, but she didn't move away. Progress.

They stood there watching each other. Her scent drifted over him, making him aware of his desire for her, any time and anywhere. She'd spent many hours in his arms and in his bed, many hours with him deep inside her. He could sense longing building within her as well. Trying to keep his need at bay, he prodded her again. "Brandi?"

"Yes. I love you with my whole heart. But…"

"Nothing else is as important." Even as he spoke, relieved by her answer, he took her hand and pulled her with him to the window seat. She didn't try to stop him and gave a small sigh.

Brandi was over his knee before she could even think of resisting. She already felt better. Colby had come to her as she'd asked, even when he should be getting ready now…just as she should be. He put her needs above everything else. That said a lot about the man she was marrying. Their marital life ahead might have ups and downs, clashes and make-ups, but she was pretty sure they would make it. Statistics weren't in their favor, though. But this was their wedding day; statistics had no place in it.

She settled into place, to heck with stupid statistics. "What if someone looks up and sees us?" They were in front of the window.

He tugged her closer. "Nobody is going to see us."

Probably not, since they were seated. "You're going to wrinkle your tux pants." Now that she was in this familiar position, she was embarrassed by her strange show of nerves. She wanted to marry this man. She really did. God, why was she so upset? Why couldn't she just go through with this?

"My pants will be fine." He didn't sound the least bit concerned. He swatted her denim-covered bottom. "You need settling down. The stress of the wedding has gotten to you, hasn't it?"

The smack over the denim hadn't hurt, but if he spanked her long enough, she knew it would eventually. "I'm a grown woman; I shouldn't be getting a little nuts about this…about wedding vows." She flinched as she watched his hand rise and fall again.

Colby's expression showed both understanding and determination. She turned her head away. She was getting spanked. Good? Bad?

"We are getting married today, Brandi Lynn." There was no question about it in his tone. He landed six sharp swats with attention-getting force. "I know you don't want to call this off." A dozen swats followed. "Do you?"

"No, but…" She gasped, her bottom hurt now. "You're sure you don't have any doubts?" She drew in a breath at a hard swat. "I won't always agree with you. I argue. I—"

He sent another biting swat down and laid his hand over the spot as if holding in the sting. "I've never had any doubts, Brandi Lynn. And I don't expect you to never argue with me. That wouldn't be who you are."

She looked back at him again. Her bottom ached, but the look of love in his eyes made up for the pain he'd caused. "So, are we done now?"

"Are you sure?" His fingers moved to the waistband of her jeans.

She trembled in response; yearning took away any wounded feelings from being spanked.

"These can come down. I can warm your bare bottom until you're convinced I will always take care of you…no matter what you need… or when."

"I'm pretty sure I get that now." She wiggled her bottom, experienced the sting beneath the denim. "No, I'm good with what you've already given me."

He smoothed his hand over her tender bottom and released her. Then as she scrambled off his lap, he said, "So, we're beyond any problems with the whole obey thing?"

"For the most part, yes."

She stood in front of him, rubbing her bottom. He frowned. "I mean that I'll try to follow those rules we've talked about. But we both know I'll struggle. Can you accept that?"

Colby watched her hands moving over her bottom. Normally he didn't allow it. Now he appeared fascinated by the action, his nostrils flaring and his eyes darkening. More than anything she wanted to pull the jeans off and….

"Colby?" she questioned, taming her thoughts. Both of them needed something, relief of some kind. She didn't want to get too disheveled and have to face her bridesmaids. Which left taking care of the man she loved. "Colby," she repeated, dropping her hands.

He looked confused, then went back to her mention of his acceptance. Still a bit distracted, he said, "As long as you're my wife, I'll accept anything." His gaze held hers. "I might spank you, but that has nothing to do with my love for you. Or everything to do with it."

Her buttocks clenched and she drew in a shuddery breath. She stepped closer to him and he hugged her as she repeated what he'd told her before, "You spank me because you love me."

She felt the pounding of his heart, the gentleness in his embrace. The scent of his arousal drifted to her and the bulge in his tux pants pressed closer.

"Sweetheart, you need to step away from me," he said huskily, although he still held her and rubbed against her to make sure she understood his problem.

She definitely did. With a smile, she reached down to cup him. She moved her hand up and down the impressive length. He shoved forward with a groan, making her smile bigger.

"Damn, Brandi Lynn, you're killing me." Yet he didn't move away, just let her have her way with him.

It always pleased her when she made him hard like this. Stepping back, she went to her knees and unzipped his pants at the same time. She drew out the heated shaft, eager to play with it.

His eyes were dark, brow pinched as he glanced toward the door. "You should be getting dressed," he managed to grunt out while she licked the head of his cock.

"I will." She licked him again, grinned at his groan and looked up. "Pretty soon." She held him with one hand and ran her tongue along one side of the pulsing shaft, following the vein line. Her other hand cupped his balls, massaged them with gentleness.

"God, Brandi," he moaned, thrusting forward, demanding more of the pleasure making him grimace with tension. "This isn't right." He moaned again. "It's damn naughty, here in church."

She leaned back and her hands continued to drive her man toward release. "Showing my future husband how much I love him is bad?"

"It's the timing that's bad," he gritted out. "Oh God! Ohhhhh God!"

Brandi worked him until he shot all over her hand. She made sure the semen stayed off his tux pants. Still holding him, she reached her other hand out to a box of tissues and cleaned him up.

"Feeling less tense now?" She smiled in mischief, very pleased with herself while he straightened his clothing.

"Hell, yes." Colby pulled her to him and kissed the top of her head. He threaded his fingers through her chin-length hair the way he liked to do sometimes. "Darlin', you don't have to promise before God and all that you will obey me. And I won't ask you to do so without good reason."

She felt way beyond foolish about the issue now, embarrassed at her breakdown. She hugged him tighter.

A second later, she shoved out of his embrace and glanced toward her dress hanging across the room. "Can you find the girls for me? I'm going to need help getting into the gown."

He stood, studied her, and nodded. "You're settled now, I take it?"

She put a hand on her tender bottom. "Yes, thank you."

"All right, I'll go round up your girls." He headed for the door, stopping to say, "I suspect it was better that I came to talk to you than your father. But you're mine now. I'll be the only one turning your sweet bottom red on occasion from now on."

***

Forty-five minutes later Colby's heart swelled with pride as he stood at the front of the church and took Brandi Lynn Dalton for his wife. Her bottom wouldn't be red by now, maybe a bit pink. Knowing their little secret about that and about what she'd done in return, he grinned like a love-struck idiot at her. He didn't care. He did love her. Even more when she met his eyes and said, "…to love, honor and obey…"

Even as he spotted her crossed fingers beneath the bouquet she held, he winked at her, lifting one eyebrow.

She blushed and let him see the crossed fingers better.

Chapter Two
Misbehavin' in Mexico

"The sun's up and we shouldn't be wasting time here in our room," Brandi said, nudging Colby where he still lay half-awake in bed. "We've only got six days here. I don't want to waste a second."

He groaned in answer, but that was it.

She was excited to be away from her accounting business, away from her clients and the demands of her new husband's ranch. Time alone with Colby was precious. He'd wanted to spend their honeymoon in Kansas City, close to home in case he was needed. She hadn't wanted that at all. She'd had to do some persuading—she'd enjoyed every delicious second—but he had given in.

She glanced at him, shivering at knowing he belonged to her. Only her. It wasn't wrong to want time away from their everyday world to get to know each other much, much better. When she'd seen an ad about Cozumel, she'd made an instant decision: that was where she wanted to go. It would be nothing at all like Kansas. He'd agreed but had shopped around online for the best deal. Besides that, he insisted she not go all crazy with overspending on trinkets.

"We already have more than enough bits of girly stuff sitting around collecting dust." The words had rankled, knowing he referred to the numerous small collections that had belonged to her mother. He hadn't been thrilled when her father let her take them to his very minimalistic house. She'd huffed at him in annoyance about his warning for their trip. But she would try to keep her impulsive buying to a minimum.

It wasn't that they were close on money. The ranch was paid for and he had a good chunk of savings and investments. And she had a nice size inheritance she could draw from. He was just Mr. Conservative and determined about the matter. She was an accountant and paid close attention to the spending habits of her clients for their businesses. She didn't overspend for her business, either. Personally, though, she hated budgets. Colby stuck to them.

She imagined they would have a lot of disagreements about budgets in their marriage. She wouldn't win them all, but some would be good. They'd already had a small disagreement about how much she'd spent on new clothes for the honeymoon. She'd "graciously" let him warm her bottom when he'd given her the choice of returning the clothes or getting spanked. Clothes were more important; her bottom recovered before too long.

"Come on, Colby," she pleaded, growing more impatient.

From his stomach down position, he turned his head and opened one chocolate brown eye to look at her. "I'm on vacation. Sleeping in is part of my dream."

He gave her a crooked grin, looking sexy as hell with his thick, black hair all mussed and the five o'clock shadow clinging to his carved face. "'Course having sex almost 24/7 this week with my new wife is a bigger part of my dream."

At his comment, spoken in his oh-so-sexy deep voice, warmth spiraled through her. Tingles down low led to moisture beading in a place that enjoyed having her husband fulfill his dreams. He'd worked hard at pleasing them both until the wee hours of the morning. Instead of feeling exhausted like him, she was flying high with energy. She wouldn't mind climbing back in bed and jumping his gorgeous bones, but she didn't want to hurt him. She had plans for him later. She'd been thinking about a certain position that seemed mighty interesting and she was pretty limber. Maybe she would let him rest after all.

"I'm afraid you're all-talk and no-can-do as far as the 24/7 sex goes." When he frowned, she smiled to let him know she was teasing. "How about we try for 20/7? I need some rest, too, my big stud muffin."

"Did I hurt you last night, sweetheart?" he asked, turning serious. "I got a bit carried away."

She fanned her face. "A bit? I lost count of my orgasms. But am I complaining? Double darn, no." She slid a long, leisurely look over the worn out cowboy. "I'll give you a break, let Mr. Wowser get back into playing condition."

Colby shifted onto his back, the sheet way down at his knees. He took hold of his semi-hard cock with one hand, making her think about reconsidering her decision. "Mr. Wowser?" he asked, stroking his shaft again and grinning while he watched her reaction.

"Yeah, got a problem with that?" She struggled, torn between the desire to sight see and the passion of taking charge of his pleasure tool

"Nah, I'm good with it. Just don't tell anyone." His gaze turned annoyed and he gave his cock one final stroke. "Like you told everyone about the damn nickname, Super Stud Cowboy."

"You already spanked me for that." She took another step back from the bed, moving her hands to cover her bottom. "I don't know why the title upsets you. It's a compliment."

He still looked unhappy. "If half the town didn't know about it, it wouldn't be so bad. But the men tease me sometimes."

Best to let the subject drop, she decided. She put her hands on her bikini-clad hips, delighted to see his eyes widen now that he noticed the scrap of fabric she was wearing. "I'm antsy. I want to go out and do something."

"I thought you were going to be on your best behavior on this trip." He sat up and moved back against the headboard.

"I haven't done anything wrong." Yet. She blew out a breath of frustration. "I just want to get out of this room. We've already been here almost solid for 24 hours."

"So you haven't been enjoying those almost 24 hours?" His testiness disappeared and he gave her a cocky grin of challenge.

She'd already learned men liked to have their egos stroked now and then. In this case, he deserved it. "You've been amazing. Super fantastic. Mind blowing magnificent. Yada, yada, yada." She focused on his cock. "It appears your brilliant woman pleaser is almost ready to dazzle me some more."

She sighed, thinking there was more to see in Cozumel, even at this resort, than just this room. "But I want to go see some sights, go to the beach, go do anything but stay here another five minutes."

"Brandi Lynn," his tone revealed how tired he was, how uncertain. He yawned, rubbed at his eyes. "You've got to be exhausted, too. You were right with me every step of the way last night."

"I'm not going to waste my day like you. I need to see what's outside this room." Before she could stop herself, she stomped her sandaled foot. "I'm leaving this room with or without you," she added more quietly, yet determined.

"Do you want to start our vacation this way?" He slipped from the bed and walked toward her, big and naked, and his eyes sparked with aggravation.

That darn foot! Always getting her into trouble. She steeled herself for confrontation. "All right, I'm sorry I stomped my foot. It was childish."

"Yes it was, Brandi Lynn. You know how I feel about your little temper tantrums." He stood in front of her, all pissed off male.

"It wasn't a tantrum," she countered. "I have an uncontrollable foot sometimes." Maybe she could distract him. Stomping her foot was one of his biggest pet peeves and she was trying to stop the habit. She reached out to smooth her hand over his chest. "Have I mentioned how much I love your pecs?"

Colby took hold of her hand. "Uh-uh. You're not going to distract me that way." His gaze shifted to her bottom. "Bend over, hands to your knees."

"Seriously? It was just a little stomp." Tears misted her eyes and she gave him a pleading look. "Please don't do this now. I'm sorry." She covered her bottom with her hands. "I've already got my bikini on to go layout for a bit and ..."

"A red bottom would be embarrassing." He drew in a breath and relented. "Okay this time, but don't do it again. Next time I'm taking off whatever shoe you have on and paddling your butt with it. Understand?"

She nodded, pulling in a breath of relief. He wasn't a cruel man by any means, but he could be focused. Part of their agreement before they'd married was that he would be the head of their household. He took his role to heart. He'd been helping her change some bad habits. She was okay with it, even though sometimes her bottom paid a price when she failed. This had been a minor mess up, made worse because he was tired.

Time to get out of the room and let him get some more rest. She moved toward the table where she'd dropped her beach towel and sunglasses. "I'll just go find a chaise on the beach to sun on until you're ready to do something else."

He pulled her close before she could dash out the door. His erection pressed against her, thick and hard, pulsing. She shivered in his embrace and smiled when he kissed the top of her head. Then he took the towel and sunglasses from her and tossed them to the floor. Neither spoke as he walked her backward across the room until she stood against the wall.

Her heart raced, anticipation thrummed through her. She liked this aggressive side of him, this I-want-you-right-damn-now side. Because she wanted the same thing.

"I've changed my mind about letting you leave right now." He cupped her head with his hands, bent down until he could kiss a favored spot on the side of her neck. "I'm going to have a little fun first." He reached between them and molded her hand around his cock. "Mr. Wowser wants some action."

He leaned back to look at her. "And that is the last time I'm calling my dick that."

She didn't care. All she cared about at the moment was how he'd begun nibbling her ear lobe behind her chin-length hair, kissing the sensitive spot beside it. She trailed a finger up and down his cock, beamed at the way it jerked within her grasp. "Guess I can spare a minute or two."

"It's going to be wild, darlin'." He untied first one side of her bikini bottom and then the other. The simple touch of his fingers on her skin made her pulse race, wishing he'd hurry up.

As she continued stroking him, he gritted his teeth on a groan, and untied her top as well, tossing it to the floor. When she stood as naked as he was, he reached down to run a hand between her legs. She eased them further apart in cooperation.

"Good girl," he praised, his voice gritty, needy. He spent a wicked second touching her hardened clit, playing.

She ground closer. "You naughty boy." Oh, this was heaven.

He lightly pinched the button, making her gasp. "Man, sweetheart. I'm a man."

"My mistake," she said, gasping for breath, as he continued tormenting the toy he'd found. "Man, all man."

He grinned when he pulled his hand up and his fingers were wet. "I'm glad I didn't let you get away too soon."

She circled her arms around his neck and rose up on tiptoes. "Is this the best you can do, cowboy?"

"Bossy woman." He smacked her bottom once and then reached down to lift her right leg up high. His cockhead nuzzled her swollen lips. "I can do better. But I don't think I can handle much foreplay right now."

"Foreplay is overrated." Brandi pulled herself up higher and seated herself on him. "Oh, yes, exactly what I needed."

Colby grimaced as she lifted up so she almost slid off and then drove back down again. He continued holding her right leg high which made her squeeze him tighter as she moved. "Thought you were in a hurry to get out of here," he teased.

She squeezed him, moved her body to circle slowly on his rod. Leaning her head back as the sensations grew, she gasped, "A few more minutes won't hurt."

His tongue found her neck, licked just under her chin. At the same time he held her in place. His hips surged forward, impaled his cock deeper and deeper. She met each of his drives, savored each one. She was hot all over; he was sweating and grunting from the effort. Neither could stop moving, both searching for that place where all thought disappeared.

Her clit hardened more and more with each piston of his cock sliding by it. The little jewel was so hard it almost hurt. She was wet and slick as he jammed into her. Drive after drive. She couldn't breathe, couldn't think, and could only feel. Then it was there, that moment of agonized ecstasy.

"Oh Colby! Oh God!" She clung to him in desperation as he pried the climax from her, all the while thrusting upward over and over. When she was finished, she leant on him, limp and drained. Still he held her. His face mirrored intense need, his jaw tight. His hips bucked as he rode harder, deeper. Seconds later he grunted out her name and ejaculated in a hot rush.

Slowly he eased her to her feet and they stood there forehead to forehead while the world steadied around them.

At last he stepped away from her and flashed a very satisfied male grin. "Okay, you can go lounge about now. I'm plum worn out." He reached down to pick up her bikini and handed the pieces to her. He was still pulling in ragged breaths. "Thanks for obliging this ole cowboy's need of his woman."

"Anytime, cowboy, anytime." She gave him a cheeky grin and dashed into the bathroom for a quick cleanup and tied her bikini back on.

When she came out again, he handed her the towel and sunglasses. "Don't wander off, darlin'. Stay on the beach. I haven't had a look around yet and I want to make sure you're safe." He gave her a light swat to her bottom. "I mean it."

She rolled her eyes, but resisted telling him that she could take care of herself. He liked taking care of her and she didn't mind, sometimes. "No problem. I want to get started on a good tan. Just don't make me stay there too long, or I'll burn."

"Half hour tops, but stay put."

Brandi hurried out, knowing it would be more like an hour at the earliest before he'd come for her. He wasn't the fastest shower taker and shaver in the world. Still, it was early in the day and with her sunscreen she would be fine.

***

Brandi watched yet another parasailer go by, followed by two jet skiers. Down the beach a group was getting ready to leave for a snorkel cruise. Another group behind her was donning fins to snorkel in the water by the nearby pier. Everyone but her was having a good time. She'd been here tanning and waiting for Colby for well over an hour. Well, she'd been patient enough!

She stood, grabbed her towel and headed for the activity booth. A tingle of unease crept up her spine, but she ignored it and walked to the smiling Mexican working there and asked, "Is it too late to rent a snorkel set and fins?" She'd never snorkeled before, but how hard could it be? No one she'd watched seemed to have any problem.

Grinning even more, the much shorter man reached behind the counter and pulled up just what she'd asked for. "Room number?"

She hesitated a second, wondering if she was being too impulsive. Colby wouldn't like her going off by herself. But she wasn't going off by herself. She planned to snorkel around the other guests. Besides, she'd probably be done and back sunning long before he managed to make it down here to the beach. What the heck was holding him up anyway? No doubt he'd gotten another stupid call from Thad with another issue at the ranch. His partner had already called two times since they'd gotten here.

"1114," she said, taking the items, and then turning to find the people she'd spotted earlier.

Where the hell is she? Colby was not happy about coming all the way down here to the beach and not finding his wife. He should have known she wouldn't stay put. Yes, he'd taken a little longer than he'd planned to because of the call from Thad, but he'd told her not to wander off. This was a strange place and there were too damn many men hanging around the hotel—even if most seemed to be with their wife or mate. Why the hell had he allowed her to wear that bikini? Why hadn't he insisted on something one piece, something without a low back or plunging neckline? Maybe one of those ankle-length sundresses he'd seen an older woman wearing as he'd walked through the hotel lobby.

He shook his head. Okay, he was being silly. She was a good-looking woman, but she didn't flaunt herself for anyone other than him. Thank God. He was just acting crazy because he couldn't find her.

Angling one hand to shade his eyes, he scanned the beach area once more. Not one sunbather. Damn.

He started to turn away when he caught sight of two patches of hot pink bobbing in the water near the pier. His gut tightened and he headed closer. The hot pink patches he saw were definitely a bikini. He tensed when he realized it was Brandi…and she was snorkeling.

Alone.

His heart pounded as he strode toward the edge of the water. As far as he knew, she'd never gone snorkeling before. She didn't even swim well. Yet she was out there in who knew how deep water—alone! He was going to roast her butt!

A minute later she dog paddled in the water and looked toward shore. He knew the instant she spotted him. She floundered a second, then righted herself and shoved off her mask and spit out the snorkel to choke out saltwater. He stood; legs planted wide apart, body rigid with fury, as she made her way out of the water.

Doing an awkward one-legged stand to remove her fins, she gave him a weak smile.

He didn't return it. "We're going back up to our room for a while, Brandi Lynn Pennington."

She blushed and removed the other fin. "I waited a long time."

"Not long enough." Colby stepped into the shallow water and took the fins, then latched onto her hand and tugged her behind him. "I distinctly remember telling you to stay put. Not to wander off." He glanced back at her. "You scared the hell out of me."

"I didn't mean to," she said, her tone sincere and tinged with regret.

In spite of the fins and snorkel gear they were holding, he drew her to him and hugged her close. A shudder went through him at how worried he'd been. "If something had happened to you…" He hugged her again before releasing her.

They dropped off the snorkel equipment and walked without speaking through the beach area, through the lobby, down the long hallway, and all the way to their secluded suite on the top floor of the hotel. Neither said a word even as they walked into the suite and Colby shut the door.

Her nerves tingling, Brandi waited as her husband glanced around the rooms. Finally, he moved to the Spanish-style sofa and sat down right in the middle. She started toward him, but he held up a hand to stop her and said, "Bring the brush."

The brush! She wanted to refuse. She'd prefer getting a spanking, a nice simple hand spanking. But then she'd not only disobeyed him but she'd also been caught in the water alone. Colby had hard and fast rules when it came to water safety, especially with her since he knew she couldn't swim. She'd broken those rules. She'd made a decision to do something just because it seemed like fun. She'd been both bored and irritated with him for not coming to find her. She wasn't a child or a young adult anymore. She was a grown up woman who ran a business and joined a man in marriage. It was time she acted more responsible.

Angry with herself more than him, she went into the adjoining bathroom and found her large, wooden hairbrush. She should have left the stupid thing home.

As she approached, Colby patted his leg. He took the brush and set it down, nodding. "You know what to do."

She hesitated, worrying her lip a second and studying his khaki shorts. "I'm wet. I'll…."

"Okay, take off the bikini."

She thought about turning away to do so, then realized how stupid that was. Still, her face heated as she untied the bottom, let it drop to the floor and then removed the top as well. She stood naked before him about to be spanked and ashamed that she deserved it.

"Stretch over, sweetheart," he said, his voice husky, which made her feel somewhat better. At least her being naked was affecting him. Not enough to change his mind, though.

She crawled onto the leather sofa by his right side and slid across his lap. The mixed feel of his cotton shorts and hairy thighs seemed odd beneath the bare skin of her abdomen. The leather felt cool against her legs and arms as she stretched out. If only they were going to do something else here, something much more enjoyable.

He nudged her forward until her bottom was in the spot he preferred on his right thigh. "You might want to grab hold of the cushion," he said, "because this is going to sting."

A warning like that was never good. In a flash, she latched onto the cushion in front of her and dug her toes into the one behind her. Her buttocks clenched, then she forced herself to relax them, knowing it hurt a whole lot more if she was tense. Before she could take another breath, it started.

Colby's hand connected with her bottom in a steady rain, a biting downpour of pain. No warm up this time. She squirmed and dug her toes in further, hissing under her breath. He meant business.

"I was hoping not to have to spank you at all on this trip." Eight sizzling smacks landed on her sit spot. "But you just can't seem to stay out of trouble. This time something bad could have happened. I could have…."

She heard him pull in a deep breath, knew he was trying to calm down. She hated that she'd frightened him. If the situation had been reversed, if he'd been the one to do something potentially dangerous, she would have been every bit as frustrated.

"I'm so sorry," she whimpered, braced to accept whatever he needed to do.

Another dozen smacks sailed onto her quivering buttocks. "You mean so damn much to me," he gritted out, smoothing his hand over her burning bottom.

She sucked in a sharp breath and dashed at her tears as he stopped to pick up the brush. "I can't seem to help myself," she gasped out. "I got bored, acted foolishly."

"You'll think before you do something so dangerous again. I guaran-damn-te it." The first swat landed in the middle of her right cheek with a resounding crack!

She yelped, arching backward. "Oh! That hurts!"

He pushed her into place again. "I reckon it does."

The brush whacked down on her blazing bottom over and over and over. All she could do was suck in frantic gasps, only to hiss a second later. It was impossible to lie still. She wriggled from side to side and began kicking up her legs.

"I'll think first." She squirmed at another smack. "I promise!"

One more swat landed and he held the brush against the underside of her buttocks. "We're done here. You've been punished for your foolishness."

"Yes," she whimpered, sniffling back tears. He hadn't spanked her this hard in a long time, not since he'd caught her driving to his place drunk after her bachelorette party. She'd earned that spanking, too.

"You'll be spending the afternoon here in the room recovering." He lifted the brush and threw it on the tiled floor. He feathered his fingers over her throbbing bottom. "Such a pretty color of red. Hot, too."

Any other time she would have enjoyed his gentle touch. Now she squirmed in discomfort. "I hate wasting time recovering."

His hand settled with firmness in warning. "Are you going to go against me again, sweetheart?"

"No," she grumped.

"Wise decision." He removed his hand. "While you're getting over this little reminder business, I'll be down on the beach, enjoying a few drinks and reading a good book."

"That's so unfair!"

"Not my fault you got your butt burned."

She snorted. "It kind of is."

A low rumble of laughter escaped him. "I guess you're right. Still, you earned it." He grew serious, helping her to stand. He took her hands to keep her standing in front of him. His eyes held warmth. "You scared me, sweetheart."

Her bottom was on fire, but the need to make love with the man who'd set it ablaze was almost overpowering. They were going to have their differences during their marriage. No doubt she'd suffer a trillion more spankings in the next fifty or so years. But they would be worth it to be married to this man who loved so deeply, who cared enough to be as patient as he could with her.

"Have I mentioned today how much I love you?" she said, inching closer to him.

Those beautiful brown eyes heated and he gave her the sexy, crooked grin that made her go weak in the knees. "No." He chuckled. "Well, you might have screamed it out a time or two this morning."

She rolled her eyes. "You're so bad, cowboy."

"Damn straight I am." He appeared to struggle with what to say next. At last he nodded toward the rumpled bed. "Go. Lie down and think about why I just roasted your sweet ass."

"Already know why," she countered, disappointed he wasn't ready to pursue what they both wanted. Still, her bottom was pretty sore. "Because you like painting my butt red." She hoped he understood she was just teasing him, not sassing him.

He did, chuckling as he headed for the door. "Red looks good on your ass. Not all the time, of course. I like it all nice and creamy, too."

"Cocky cowboy." Her cowboy and she wasn't sure she deserved him.

Stopping to glance back at her, his gaze shifted to the bulge growing in his shorts. "And I know how to use this cock, don't I, sweetheart?"

She crawled onto the bed, looked back at him on hands and knees, and wiggled her bottom at him. Like a matador waving a red flag at a bull. "You might need a little more practice before you reach perfection."

Again, he chuckled, but he didn't come to her like she'd hoped. "I'll be practicing more later. For now, you need to do some practicing of those three little words you swore to me last week." He held her gaze, amusement dancing in his eyes. "Particularly that one word you had so much trouble with. Obey."

Would he ever forget her last minute panic? Something that had resulted in her walking down the aisle with a red bottom. That spanking hadn't been as intense as this one. Thank goodness.

"I'm still working on it," she said on a sigh.

He winked at her. "And I'll be helping you get a good handle on the definition. Because I love the hell out of you, sweetheart."

Chapter Three
A Chocolate Kind of Day

Colby grabbed his cell phone from the chest of drawers and glanced out the bedroom window. Thick dark clouds swirled around a gray early July sky. The day promised to be one of those cloudy, depressing days. The kind made for grabbing his hot little wife and taking her back to bed for the entire day. She could be one delicious handful when he encouraged her to let loose her passionate nature. Lord a' mighty, she'd almost done him in on their honeymoon in Cozumel. Almost.

He forced the dream notion aside. He was already running late. The reality was he had cattle to move to another field and supplies to pick up in town. The damn list went on and on. Still, he strode through the house looking for Brandi. If nothing else maybe he'd sneak in a quickie before he had to head out the door. She was usually game for some impulsive playtime. Impulsive should have been her middle name. Although there were times when that wasn't one of her good traits.

He found her in the kitchen, loading the dishwasher with their breakfast dishes, but not paying attention to the chore. Her shoulders were tense. Something was on her mind that she didn't like and he figured he knew the issue. They should discuss it, but he didn't want to. Right now he was enticed by her pert backside and the way a pair of faded jean shorts fit it so well.

Intent on the sight, he crossed the room until he stopped behind her to squeeze her bottom. So perfect, so damn tempting.

She didn't move away, but grumbled, "I thought you were already gone."

Pissy mood, not a good sign. He squeezed her butt again and then reached up to brush aside her short auburn hair, which still annoyed him. Fingering the soft strands, he recalled the impulsive and rebellious decision she'd made a week before the wedding. She had her long, wavy blonde hair trimmed and colored red. He'd been disgusted and she'd regretted her decision. After he dried her tears, they had a discussion, which had led to a spanking...that had led to....

Led to exactly what he had in mind when he came looking for her. She stood stiff and he decided to attempt to lighten her mood. He leaned down to nuzzle the side of her neck and inhaled her familiar light floral perfume and a scent that was all Brandi. His jeans became uncomfortable in a flash.

She had only relaxed a bit. He nibbled her ear lobe and said in a gruff tone, as he toyed with her hair. "I thought you were going to get your hair dyed back to blonde."

Proving he should have left the subject alone, she jerked away to turn and glare at him. "I said I would and I will. Drop it, okay."

He raised an eyebrow at the snap in her tone. "Still upset with the change of your plans for this morning?"

Her lips pressed together and she huffed, "Yes. There are some good garage sales this weekend."

Her friend Sarah had called last night to let her know she couldn't go today. Not that he minded his wife missing out on another opportunity to pick up more stuff they didn't need around the house. But Brandi didn't like it when things didn't go her way, although eventually she adjusted. Sometimes it took a little help, like his hand applied to her butt.

"There's no use pouting because Sarah can't go, sweetheart," he said, meeting her irritated blue gaze. "She's going to have more serious things on her mind today than buying someone else's throw-outs."

"Like getting her bottom warmed, you mean? Thad could've waited until later, even tomorrow. After all Sarah dented the stupid fender three days ago."

She froze, clapped a hand over her mouth, and her cheeks grew pink. It was clear he wasn't supposed to know she'd been aware of the incident.

"So, you knew about it all along? Didn't bother to tell me." His partner, Sarah's fiancé, had loaned Sarah his pickup truck before he went out of town to a cattlemen's meeting in Dodge City. She'd had a fender-bender, a small one, but she'd tried to get it fixed—unsuccessfully—before he returned and then not told him about it. Thad had been furious, at the not telling him about the dent and just letting him discover it. Colby would have felt the same way.

"She's my friend! I wouldn't tattle on her." Brandi's stubborn chin jutted out.

"He's my friend and he had a right to know. Now the insurance won't pay for the repair because it wasn't reported right away and too long a time has lapsed." The real issue was Sarah had tried to keep the whole thing a secret.

Brandi avoided his gaze. "She was trying to get it repaired; trying to make it so Thad would never know she'd damaged his truck. I would have done the same thing." Again, she clamped a hand over her mouth and flushed even more.

"Turn around, Brandi Lynn." That was what he'd figured. Dammit. He wanted to nip this issue, and any future issue about anything to do with lying or keeping secrets, right in the bud.

As he expected, she didn't obey him. She was still struggling with the word, the concept. It had almost been a deal breaker on their wedding day.

"Don't you have cattle to move? Or supplies to go into Hinkley for?" she countered, not moving an inch.

He wasn't letting this go and her being stubborn wasn't helping any. "Brandi Lynn," he repeated, his whole body stiffening from the strain of the situation. "This won't take long."

"Why are you so pigheaded determined about this? Can't we agree to disagree?"

"Sweetheart, I understand having your friend's back, but you need to know when that's a good decision…and when it's not." He pulled in a breath to steady his sour attitude. "You know what the real problem is, don't you?"

She clenched her jaw and took a second before she nodded, her shoulders slumping. "You think I lied to you, but I didn't. I just didn't come forth with an unfortunate bit of information. What happened had nothing to do with us."

"Tomato, tomatoe, sweetheart." He motioned with a finger for her to turn around.

"Difference of interpretation. I get that." She shot him an annoyed look and started to turn toward the counter. "Sarah is the one who—"

"Did wrong? Yes," he cut her off. "Is getting her butt burned this morning, yes." He glanced toward the counter, frowning. "Her accomplice to the crime is about to pay her dues as well."

She mumbled something under her breath, which irritated him even more. "I'm sure you didn't just call me a bad name, right?"

When she blew out a deep breath and refused to look at him, he had his answer. Sometimes she didn't know when to pick her fights. Getting all prickly and sassy was a bad choice given the situation.

"Just do it, okay? I screwed up and I admit it. I knew it was wrong at the time, but…." She looked over her shoulder at him, resignation in her expression. "In a way I'm glad we're dealing with this. The burden of the secret was becoming kind of heavy."

Colby was proud of her for acknowledging her mistake, but it didn't mean he was going to change his mind about this. He put a hand to her back and bent her over further. "I don't like having to punish you, sweetheart. But what you did was unacceptable behavior. It makes you untrustworthy."

Untrustworthy? Now she felt miserable. Getting spanked would be bad enough, but for him to not believe he could trust her… Well, that was huge. Tears misted her eyes as she looked over her shoulder to face him. His expression held disappointment. This had to be fixed.

It took some serious bucking up, but she shifted her gaze to the crock of utensils next to the stove. She couldn't say the words, hoped he understood her message. He did and snagged one of the wooden spoons. Her stomach tightened with dread.

He held it and she stared at the source of unpleasantness, swallowing hard.

"I asked you about the dent. You told me you had no idea what happened," he said unhappiness in his tone. "Fact is you lied to me."

She bobbed her head, unable to deny it. Good intentions on her friend's behalf or not, she'd let her husband down. Made him feel he couldn't trust her. That sickened her. She gripped the counter top on either side of her and waited with her denim-covered bottom stuck out.

If he had more time, she was sure he would have made her pull the jeans down. But his men were already waiting for him. No doubt waiting for Thad as well, because he was dealing with Sarah about now, too.

Colby still had trouble believing she'd lied to him. She knew he hated lies, wouldn't put up with them. Before they'd gotten married, they had talked about a lot of issues and their beliefs. There were ten years between them and differences in their maturity level. Brandi had been spoiled most of her life, disciplined, too. But even with that, she'd pretty much done what she pleased. He intended to be the best husband she could have and that included correcting her misbehaviors, helping her become more responsible for her actions. His role in their marriage wouldn't always be a pleasant one.

She'd promised him that she would never lie to him. Yet she had. For a friend. The excuse of it being an error of omission wasn't good enough. Resigned to what he believed necessary, he shoved her T-shirt onto her back. "We've discussed the importance of trust in a marriage, haven't we? And lying, too?" It was important to reiterate why this was being done.

"Yes." Her response was quiet.

He swatted her butt once, hard, with his hand. "Abusing trust in a relationship can hurt it, drive a wedge between us. I don't want that. You said you didn't want that either. Right?" He held his hand still against her taut ass.

Her buttocks clenched and unclenched. "Right. I love you, Colby. I'm sorry."

He treasured her words of love, but knew she expected him to take charge now. "Yet you chose to essentially lie to me." He spanked her in a quick rain of biting smacks that stung his hand as well.

She glanced back at him, gave him an apologetic look, and faced the counter again. "I disappointed you, let both of us down."

When she lowered her head, he understood that was her sign of acceptance. She was ready. He wanted this over with. He picked up the spoon he'd set on the counter and wasted no time in placing a dozen quick, attention-getting swats on her butt. Even through the denim they were hard enough that she danced up on her toes and hissed.

He held the spoon at the under-curve of her ass, watched her tense again. He was almost done. "Ready to finish this?"

"Yes," she whispered, bracing her arms again.

He almost changed his mind, but she was waiting for him, willing to accept what he believed necessary. He couldn't let her down. Steeling himself, he landed a baker's dozen of thirteen smacks on her wriggling butt. The final three right to her sit spot. She would think about this incident every time she sat down today.

Relieved, he stepped back. "We're done."

"I got the message," she said on a whimper. "The spoon delivers a nasty sting."

After sitting the spoon on the counter, he eased her shirt back down. He shifted her around until she looked at him again, an embarrassed heat warming her face, tears trickling down her cheeks. "I love you, sweetheart."

Brandi blinked away tears, gave a weak smile. "I know you do."

The sadness in her voice drew him closer. He tugged her into his embrace, unconcerned she was rubbing her ass to ease the throbbing. He lowered his head and she met him halfway for the kiss they both wanted. Her softness got to him as it always did. The scent of her teased his senses, as did the lingering smell from their earlier lovemaking. The combination made him rock hard. But he didn't have time to shuck his pants and take her right now, so he made love to her mouth instead.

She appeared to forget about having gotten spanked and melted into him. That little tongue of hers slipped out and moved feather-soft across his lips. With a moan of desire, she went up on her toes, locked her arms around his neck, and gave in to the kiss. Their tongues danced and their mouths mated until they both were panting. When he began thrusting his hips forward and feared he was about to come right in his jeans, he broke away and stepped back.

His chest rose and fell as he grabbed up deep, steadying breaths. She, too, leaned back against the counter, grimaced a second, and then sucked in air. Her eyes pleaded for more, but he shook his head.

"I would if I could, but the men are waiting for me." All he could do was adjust his uncomfortable jeans and head for the back door. "It's damn hard to walk away, damn hard."

"Stupid cattle," she grumbled.

He faced her at the last minute, chuckled at her pouty expression. It was a struggle not to change his mind and just stay with her. But his ranch needed him and she had other things to do as well. "When you get over feeling sorry for yourself, you can work on the ranch books, here or at your office. Or you can paint the spare bedroom like you've been talking about," he reminded her.

When she stood there rubbing her butt, still frustrated that he was leaving, he added, "Or you can go back up to the bedroom and stay there for the day."

Her eyes widened. "As in you'd confine me to my room? Like a child?"

He shrugged. "Unless you're going to deal with your sore butt and move on that seems like a good option."

She snorted. "It's not an option. I'll find something to do."

***

By noon, Brandi had talked with Sarah and they'd commiserated over their trials with the men they loved, although Sarah had suffered much more at her fiancé's hands than Brandi had. Still, Sarah was confined to the house they shared for the weekend. This meant no shopping together, no going to a movie together, nada.

By one, Brandi had dusted most of the large log home and run the vacuum cleaner. She'd even tossed in a load of laundry. After that she decided to attack the storage closet, which had been stuffed to the ceiling with junk. That's where she found the box of Godiva chocolates she'd splurged on a couple of months ago and hidden away because Colby knew eating chocolate affected her like no other sweet. She'd get a sugar rush so high she'd act like a crazy person, adrenalized into endless action. Her doctor had told her not long ago that she was entering the borderline stage of diabetes. She promised her doctor, herself, and Colby that she'd watch her diet better, especially her sugar—including chocolate—consumption. But it was a struggle.

Feeling like a kid at Christmas, she carried her unearthed treasure upstairs to their bedroom. She sat down in the middle of the king sized bed, turned on the TV to watch a "chick flick" as Colby called the romance she'd recorded last week, and opened the box of chocolates. She would finish up the closet later. It was time to pamper herself a little, with a movie and chocolate. She'd only eat one or two pieces and her husband would never have to know. The box would be hidden once more before he returned this evening. One or two pieces wouldn't be a big deal. It was cheating, yes, but just a little.

***

Colby dragged himself into the house at six o'clock. Every muscle in his body screamed in pain. Damn runaway heifer! She'd slipped away from the rest of the herd and run like the wind. He'd gone after her and managed to get thrown off his horse when it had spotted a snake and reared up. He'd gotten his bruised body back into the saddle and managed to get the heifer back with the herd. Now all he wanted was a long, hot soak in the shower, and then he'd collapse on the sofa to watch a ballgame. He'd sweet talk Brandi into fixing him a sandwich and maybe even massaging his back. He'd told her at breakfast not to worry about fixing supper tonight because he hadn't known when he'd get home.

Walking from the kitchen into the living room, he stopped and gaped. What the hell had she been up to? The doors of the entertainment center were open and every one of their far too many DVDs were stacked in front of it. His golf bag sat a few feet away, something he rarely got to use. His clubs laid scattered about on the floor beside the bag, cleaning wax and a cloth nestled among them. And the storage closet was open and empty. Every item that had been crammed inside it lay around the jumble of stuff, as if someone had started sorting through it and stopped.

Confused, he wasn't sure how to react. Interrupting his thoughts, he heard footsteps upstairs in the bedroom, and then they moved down the hallway toward the stairs. He watched as Brandi stopped at the top of the staircase, her arms full of clothes. Then, with a muffled grunt, she tossed her burden over the railing. A rain of clothing fell to the floor six feet from where he stood.

"Oh, good, you're home," she said in forced happiness, reaching to shove a lock of short hair behind an ear. "There's a whole other pile to be carried down here."

Colby doubted he could even lift a feather at the moment, even if he wanted to—which he didn't. He motioned to the scattered faded jeans, ancient T-shirts, and his old ratty-looking-but-much-loved college sweatshirt. "Just what's going on, sweetheart?"

She shook her head at him as if he were dimwitted. "What does it look like? I'm cleaning out things."

"Now? Why the hell are you doing this right now?" he grumbled, taking a second look at her. Was that a spot of chocolate on her chin? He discarded the thought.

They'd discussed, thoroughly, how chocolate was bad for her last Easter, when she'd eaten a half dozen chocolate-covered marshmallow eggs from her niece's Easter basket. She'd buzzed around the house after they'd come home from her brother's like a wild bee. Searching for things to do. Cleaning kitchen cabinets with endless enthusiasm, waxing their no-wax floor with some old wax she'd found in the garage. That had been tough to get off, but necessary before it damaged the expensive new floorcovering. Plus there was the newest scare: her becoming a diabetic.

When he looked closer, he noticed her eyes appeared more glazed than they should. Damn. He recognized the sign of a sugar high. Anger and worry battled within him. He stormed up the stairs as she disappeared into the bedroom again. She was risking her health. She could be taking years off her life and he damn well wanted her to live a good long time.

When he entered the room, he found her bent over nose-to-floor, grabbing shoes from the closet. One glance at the bed and the crumpled candy wrappers beside the almost empty Godiva chocolate box told him she'd ignored her promise of eating no more chocolate. Fear of losing her too soon pinched at his heart. His hand itched to connect with the saucy little butt wiggling a few feet away.

Unable to resist the temptation, he walked up behind her and gave her bottom a solid smack!

Brandi jerked upright, a hand shooting back to rub at the sting, and spun to glare at him. "What was that for?" Her eyes sparked in outrage.

"Have you done something today you weren't supposed to do?" he prodded, thinking about the mess in the living room and here, too, and even more about the sugar issue.

She frowned at him, crinkling her nose. "You're sweaty, you smell like a horse. Go take a shower and leave me to my work."

"Brandi Lynn," he warned. "I know you well enough to know cleaning closets isn't something you do very often. Certainly not with the kind of gusto you displayed by the mess you've made all over the house."

She started to turn away, muttering, "The time just seemed right. No big deal." She bent again for the shoes, waving him away. "Go on, leave me alone or I'll never get done in here. And I'm going to work on your den after this."

"Not in this lifetime!" he countered, knowing it was time to take some action. He grabbed her by the waist and pulled her out of the closet. "We're going to have us a little lesson about the importance of standing behind a promise."

Brandi tried to get free, dropping the load of shoes in her arms. For a split second, she glowered at him, and then she spotted the candy wrappers and box of chocolate, incriminating evidence of her misbehavior. Eyes downcast, she reached up to wipe around her mouth, no doubt trying to make sure there was no additional damning evidence of her blatant act of disobedience.

"Promise?" she questioned quietly.

"I'm not blind. I noticed the whirlwind of activity you attempted downstairs. From a sugar rush." He drew in a tense breath. "And I see the candy wrappers on the bed."

She worried her lower lip, guilt heavy in her expression when she glanced at him.

When she didn't say anything, he clarified, "Chocolate. You promised not to touch it, let alone eat it. At least in large quantities. Or any other sugar, for that matter."

She studied the carpet. "I only meant to eat a couple of pieces."

"Were you even supposed to have it in the house?" They'd talked about all of this after that fateful doctor's appointment. He well remembered the fear that had grabbed hold of him. He didn't want to lose her for a very long time. He would rather die first.

She raised her head. "No."

Colby refused to back down even though he could see her regret. "Why did we make the agreement?"

"Because I go a little crazy," she mumbled.

He motioned toward the closet and the cleaned out dresser drawers, their contents spread out on the floor. "Did you go a 'little crazy'?"

"I guess so." It looked like the sugar rush had ended and she said on a heavy sigh, "It's going to take hours to clean this back up."

"That it will, sweetheart. That it will. Tomorrow."

He knew he should warm her ass and he could see she expected him to do just that. But he'd already smacked her bottom earlier with the spoon. He was pretty sure she'd suffered some from that biting sting. Not enough to keep her out of trouble all day, though. Still, he was torn about what he needed to do in regard to this particular problem.

Brandi looked at him in wariness, waiting. He leaned down to pick up one of her house slippers. It had a nice thick, rubber sole.

Her eyes narrowed in on the slipper. "Are you going to…?"

He should, but he wasn't. Tossing down the slipper, he shook his head. "No, although you sure have earned another butt warming."

Brandi stared at him, relief sweeping over her. She thought about the storage shed and the way she'd taken all the gardening tools and other tools off the shelves. They were in a pile on the floor, waiting for her to come back and reorganize them. All she'd done today was create one mess after another. With each one, she'd planned to go back later and put things in their proper places. Colby would have a hissy fit when he discovered the shed's pile. She'd get spanked for sure then.

"I'm so sorry," she apologized, wanting to go to him and have him take her in his arms. She needed him in so many ways. Sometimes as her disciplinarian. More as simply the man who loved her, comforted her, forgave her when she disappointed him.

As if he read her mind, he walked right in front of her. He rubbed a thumb at a spot where she'd failed to get rid of some evidence of her error in judgment. "If there's any chocolate left, I'm tossing it in the trash."

Meeting his troubled gaze, she nodded, grateful that would be her punishment this time. Even though she'd known it had been wrong to give in to the urge, the chocolate had tasted so good. At first. Then she'd started feeling guilty about eating it, but she hadn't been able to put the box away. "I was weak. Chocolate is my drug of choice. I guess I'm addicted."

His arms encircled her as he pulled her close until she pressed her head against his chest. "We'll get you through your chocolate withdrawal, sweetheart. I'll always have your back." He kissed the top of her head, fingered her hair as he'd done earlier. His heart pounded against her ear and she heard the deep rumble of his voice when he added, "I'm beginning not to hate this short cut. But I prefer you as a blonde."

"First thing next week I'll make an appointment with my beautician," she vowed.

"Good." He held her a second longer before he eased her back so she could look up at him. His expression was serious, his eyes filled with concern. "You know what the doctor said. I know what she said."

Her shoulders slumped, realizing this had been another incident that would make him less able to trust her. Again, she felt sick by that awareness. "I try hard most of the time." She blinked back a tear. "I keep letting you down and I'm so very sorry."

He smoothed his hand over her back. "Everyone has a moment of weakness now and then. I understand that. In your situation, you need to be more careful." His jaw tightened. "The problem was you went crazy with it. You had no self-control. And that's what's dangerous."

He was right. Why couldn't she be more responsible? Like him. She'd never seen him act foolish. She wanted to make him proud of her, wanted to be a good wife. Which made her think about their long talks before they'd got married and about their agreements between one another.

She pulled in a breath to steady her nerves. "We agreed you'd spank me when I went against the doctor's warning. And I went way past it this afternoon."

"I remember what I promised, but I also have the right to deal with your misbehavior in other ways. I'm not going to give you a second spanking today."

Thank God. "I'll accept whatever you think is right."

His eyes warmed and the tension eased between them. "Are there any other chocolate stashes? Any other messes you've made that I should know about?"

Uh-oh. She wasn't in the clear just yet, but she had to be honest with him. "Chocolate…in the laundry room…behind the soap box."

He swatted her bottom, lightly, shaking his head. "That was for keeping chocolate stashes when you know they're forbidden."

She didn't even flinch or protest because it could have been much worse.

His big hand rested on her bottom. "Anything else you want to admit?"

She considered not telling him the rest, but that would be irresponsible. "Storage shed. Mess. But I'll clean it up."

He stiffened. "My storage shed? Haven't I told you to leave it alone?" He smacked her once, a little harder. "Damn, sweetheart."

She couldn't believe she was still standing, not being pulled across the room and planted face down over his knee. The vein pulsing in his neck told her how much his restraint was costing him.

"Are you sure you don't want to…?"

"Oh, yes, I do want to burn your ass right now," he gritted out. He didn't reach for her, though. "I'm not going to do it."

"Why not?" she asked and wondered if she was nuts. He was being lenient; she should accept his gift of love. "I screwed up, a lot."

"That you did." His gaze softened. "Part of your punishment will be cleaning it all up tomorrow. I imagine that will keep you busy for most of the day."

She didn't look forward to the task. She had a lot of messes. "Part of the punishment?" Did he intend to delay her spanking until the next day?

"The other part is that you need to go to bed early tonight. No supper. No TV."

"Like a child?" she asked in dismay. That was almost worse than getting spanked.

His whole expression changed, all signs of irritation with what she'd done disappeared. His eyes darkened. "Not like a child, sweetheart. Like a woman about to have her man take charge of her...in bed."

Okay, now that she could live with. "Have you do whatever you wanted with me?" she questioned, giving him a smile. "A decadent discipline."

The crooked grin she so loved slipped into place. "Exactly."

Her heart raced as she stepped back and motioned him toward the bathroom. "Go. Shower." She glanced at the mess on the bed. "I'll clean things up a bit."

His chest rose and fell with ragged breaths. She saw the way the front of his jeans pushed out with his growing erection. Yes, yes, yes! This promised to be a much better end to the day.

He jerked off his shirt, toed off his boots. "You'd best get to it, woman. I've got plans for my naughty wife and you'd better be waiting and ready when I come back."

She shivered at the desire in his tone. "How do you want me waiting, cowboy?"

The heat in his eyes made her want to rip off her clothes, tear off the rest of his, and shove him down to the floor. She'd be on top of him in an instant, playing cowgirl to the max. But she was determined to let him stay in control. She liked it when he got all masterly.

Tugging down his jeans and undershorts, he growled in a husky tone, "I expect to find you butt up, sweetheart."

Brandi was more than ready to "love, honor and obey" her husband of just over a month. "Yes, sir." She gave him a sassy smile that made his eyes widen and had him all but running into the bathroom for his shower.

While he was gone, she shed the rest of her clothes, tossed them with the rest of the mess in front of the closet. She picked up one side of the comforter and shook it enough to make the candy box and wrappers fly off. Then she shoved the covers to the end of the mattress before crawling across until she stretched out in the middle of the bed. The sheets felt cool and the light brush of air from the paddle fan felt good over her already heated body. Soon she hoped the room would be like an oven from the heat they'd stir up.

A few minutes later, record time for Colby, he emerged from the shower. His hair was still damp, but he'd dried off the rest of his superb body. Exhaustion was clear in the weary way he moved, until he looked at her. His eyes sparked with renewed eagerness; his cock stood out proud and long in front of him. And he hurried toward the bed.

"Is this what you wanted?" Brandi asked, all too focused on the shaft her body was desperate for.

He stroked his cock once, breathing hard. "On your hands and knees. Forehead to the mattress. I want your sweet ass up nice and high."

Her heart raced and tingles of anticipation spiraled through her, settling in her woman's place. She moved quickly into the position he'd requested.

"Spread your legs." He moved onto the bed behind her, smoothing his hands up and down the insides of her thighs, making them tremble. He touched her lower lips and he eased a finger in just enough to gather some of the moistness already there. "My woman is ready," he said in a husky tone, pleased.

She pushed her bottom up even higher, ached for him to fill her. "Yes," she purred. Would he want to play some first? She didn't need it, only wanted his big rod driving into her. When he didn't make another move, she lost her patience. She craned her head around to look at him, heart racing even more as she watched him rubbing his engorged cock. "Am I going to have to force you down and take over myself? Because I will!"

He grinned, one of those haughty men's grins. He guided his shaft to her. "I'm in charge. Got a problem with that?"

"No." She watched in fascination as he pushed the cockhead inside her and then slammed home. "Ohhh," she gasped more in relief than pain. It had only been this morning when they'd made love, but she never seemed to get enough of feeling him deep inside her. She enjoyed the experience even more now that they'd stopped using condoms because they were ready to start a family.

He pumped in deliberate slowness, holding her hips to make her stay in position. It was too slow. Need burned inside her, frustration. She looked back at him, gritting out, "Are you trying to torture me? Is this your punishment?"

His face contorted in near pain as he picked up his pace. His hips pistoned forward and his fingers gripped her hips. "I'm suffering, too." He blew out a heavy breath, drove deeper. "I'm done with that."

Immediately the steady pounding into her became frantic. Convulsions rippled through her, she squeezed her eyes shut as the tension grew and grew. Finally she exploded, gasping, crying out his name. He was right behind her. His orgasmic growl filling the room at the same time his release hit him hard.

The bed moved as he collapsed beside her and rationality found its way into her thoughts again. She loved this man with all of her heart. But she struggled with disappointing him. She'd lied to him; she'd gone behind his back with the chocolate matter. She wanted him to trust her, but she would have to earn it. Especially if she wanted to have him love her for the next sixty or more years. There were too many other women out there who would relish having a chance at her cowboy.

Not going to happen.

Chapter Four
Boredom = Trouble

Brandi glanced out the window in the dining area of the big country kitchen and barely managed to spot the sun peeking through the clouds. She yawned. This was too early for a sane person to be up, even if she'd been raised on a ranch and knew their crazy hours. As an accountant who owned her own business, her work hours were more controlled. There had been a time when she'd gone to the office whenever it pleased her, but her husband had discouraged that. They'd argued about the matter before they'd gotten married. Older and wiser—in his opinion—he'd been very persuasive. After a while, he'd convinced her that clients expected her to keep regular working hours, so they could contact her more easily. He'd been right. Her clients were happier and she was adjusting.

But this was Saturday, late August, and she didn't have to be at the office. She also didn't have anything specific that she had to get done today. So as soon as Colby stopped to give her a quick kiss goodbye as he headed out to do chores, she was going back to bed. Alone. Unfortunately.

She heaved a sigh and wiped off the table with a washrag, as the dishwasher, filled with breakfast dishes, rumbled across the room. Somehow she didn't hear her husband's boot steps as he walked up behind her. He snaked an arm around her and clamped a hand onto her left breast.

Startled, she jerked. And then smiled. The day just might get better than she'd expected.

"Sure do love these sweet handfuls," he said squeezing her breast and reaching for the other one as well. He didn't like to play favorites, or so he'd told her.

She savored the warmth of his touch, the brush of his palms over her nipples, which were hardening. She wore a short filmy nightgown but wanted even that much clothing off. It had been a few days since they'd made any kind of love, and she was more than ready!

"I've only got a few minutes," he said, moving his hands down to explore between her legs. "'Pears my hot little wife is wet and willing."

She craned her head to look back at him, giving him her most enticing smile. "Always, cowboy."

He pulled his hand away and reached to unbuckle his belt. She turned to face him, tugging off her nightgown and wiggling out of the panties. "I'm all yours."

His impressive chest rose and fell in a shuddery breath, stretching the blue chambray shirt to its limits. His chocolate eyes warmed and he drew in air through flared nostrils. Lower, his thick erection pushed at his zipper. "Damn, sweetheart, those are words I love to hear."

"Lie down for me, on your back. On the table. You know how I want you." His hands shook as he finished freeing his swollen cock.

Good thing she'd just cleaned the table. She didn't even hesitate to squirm her way on top of the cool wood surface. Holding his gaze, she lay back, making sure her bottom was close to the edge. She was all about being helpful.

He inched forward as he spread her thighs, pushing them up until her knees were bent. Grinning, he nudged her slit with the head of his cock. "Ready?"

He had to see the beads of moisture, see her trembling with desire. "What do you think?"

"That you want this rod driven deep." He held her legs as he did just that. Her groan told him she was as pleased with the experience as he was.

"Oh, yeah," she sighed. She'd take her handsome cowboy any way, any how, any time. "I'm at your mercy."

He leaned down to swirl his tongue around her belly button, making her clench tighter around his shaft. He chuckled and did it again. She clamped around him once more, pleased to hear his rumbled groan. In return, he thrust back and forth, hard and fast, before almost withdrawing.

"What are you doing?" she snapped, bucking her hips upward to force him deeper. "Teasing me?"

"You're so easy to tease." But he slid deeper again, growing still and torturing her in another way.

Slowly beginning to move again, he gave her an intense look, stopping once more. "One of these days I'd like to try something special, something daring."

Brandi trembled in anticipation and wished he'd get to it again. "Daring?" She trusted him; she would do pretty much whatever he wanted.

While their gazes locked, he licked his index finger and met her gaze in challenge. He didn't have to say anything. She knew what he had in mind. They'd talked about this during their honeymoon when they'd shared their fantasies. She hadn't been ready then, wasn't sure she was right now. But she didn't stop him.

Watching for her reaction, he eased his cock free and moved his finger toward her small hole. She held her breath. Would it hurt? Should she stop him?

Before she could make a decision, he guided his finger inside her. It didn't feel different from when her doctor did a rectal exam, except this was her husband touching her with such intimacy. She held still waiting to see what would happen next.

"Are you okay?" his concern touched her, made everything all right. He would stop if she told him to.

She nodded.

Looking pleased, he pulled the finger out, and then drove two in its place. "I don't have a lot of time. Maybe we should go back to—"

"No!" While she loved having his thick shaft inside her, she wasn't ready to stop this new experience. It felt so naughty, wicked. She clamped her inner muscles around his fingers, tingling at the strange stretching. "Don't waste time then!"

He chuckled. "All right then. You're about to get your first butt fucking. With my fingers."

She loved the deep huskiness in his tone. Liked the take-charge attitude, knowing it meant he was in a serious give-it-to-her-good mood. Her hands curled around the table edge as he worked her with care, with his fingers in her sensitive hole.

It didn't take long before she keened low in her throat and held her breath, anxious. She looked at him in desperation, wanting him to finish this.

"I'll take care of it, sweetheart." He drove his fingers in again and she gasped. As if he understood she couldn't take much more, he took her to the breaking point.

She held on to the tabletop for dear life. Suddenly an orgasm washed over her and she cried out with it. Her release coated her muff and his hand while he smiled in smugness.

"Quite a ride, huh?" he asked and pulled his fingers free. "Thanks for letting me do that."

Her heart was still pounding and she collapsed on the tabletop. He grabbed a paper towel and, with gentleness, cleaned her up, continuing to grin.

"You're proud of yourself, aren't you?" She thought maybe she should feel awkward, embarrassed, but she didn't.

He tucked his less needy cock back in place and finished righting his clothes. "Guess I am. Not every woman would let a man do that. You're damn special, sweetheart. Understanding." He snagged her gaze, looking serious. "I won't ask that of you again. I just wanted…I just needed to try it once."

She sat up, wincing, and eased off the table. "Never say never, cowboy." When he studied her in curiosity, she shrugged. "It wasn't awful. But I'll have to think about it before I'll do it again."

"Fair enough." He grabbed his hat off the counter. "See you tonight. Have yourself a good day." With a quick kiss, he strode out the back door.

Brandi stood there for several minutes, catching her breath after the surprising experience. It had been the first exciting thing to happen to her in days, in weeks. Maybe tonight….

She picked up her nightgown and put it back on. Her asshole was a bit sore, but nothing she couldn't live with. She grabbed the washrag that had fallen to the floor, re-wet it, and went back to wipe down the table again. Her pulse raced, envisioning how she'd laid there minutes ago with her husband doing some very naughty business to her. Something interesting to think about.

And that made her consider how boring her life had become, except for this brief interlude that hadn't lasted more than ten minutes.

Other than being the sexiest cowboy on earth, Colby was, for the most part, boring. Predictable. Up in the morning at 5:00am everyday without help of the alarm clock. She got up, grudgingly, to be the "good" wife and make him breakfast: eight scrambled eggs, six pieces of bacon and four pieces of toast—exactly—day after day. As soon as he snarfed that down in amazing speed, he came around the table to where she sat in an exhausted stupor and gave her a quick kiss before he grabbed his hat and headed out the door. Then she went back to bed for three or four hours.

Yes, this had been an exceptional morning.

Looking at his dishwasher chugging away, she went back to thinking about his routine. Her worn out cowboy pretty much showed up around six o'clock each night, unless there was some kind of ranching emergency or something to throw his schedule off. She'd tried to vary his basic meat-and-potatoes meals with a little Italian, some Mexican, even a bit of Chinese. He hadn't complained. But she'd gone back to simple steaks and baked potatoes and he'd been ecstatic. Boring. Done in from his physical labor-filled day and a big meal, he then liked to stretch out on the leather sofa and channel surf until ten o'clock. After that he yawned and stretched and was ready for them to go to bed. Of course, he snuggled with her for a while and even made love to her most nights. Except recently. He'd been too tired for more than a snuggle.

The oh-so-exciting life of being married to a rancher. A big ho-hum! She'd grown up on a ranch and knew what to expect, but still…

She couldn't take it anymore! Not that she wanted to get in serious trouble with Colby, but, jeez, what was the harm in just a little mischief? Besides, she'd been "good" for over a month now. After getting her bottom whacked with the wooden spoon for lying to him about Sarah's accident, she hadn't gone even another minute over his knee. Well, she'd come close with the chocolate incident. But that had worked out quite well.

She hadn't even gotten a single swat as he passed by her one time or another. Something she kind of found titillating. It was time to liven up things around here, press her boundaries a little.

She looked, without focusing, out the window again. Some parts of their life were easy, like getting chores done. She didn't do ranch chores and didn't go horseback riding unless with Colby. So, for the most part, she'd been inside, either here or at the office. She needed a change of pace.

A breeze ruffled the leaves and caught her attention. With the sun rising now, she sensed it was going to be a beautiful day. The news last night had said it would be one of those perfect early autumn days. Good for being outside, even though hot.

Smiling, she decided to snag a little more rest, maybe do some planning in her head. Then she would fill her day with anything but thinking about financial statements, client needs, or ranch accounting.

***

Two hours and some much-needed sleep later, wearing her faded jeans, Brandi stood with hands on hips and looked into the garage. This was Colby's private world and it was out of control. It needed some serious reorganization. She'd considered getting some fresh air and exercise by going jogging, but then she'd thought about the garage. He'd been intending to clean it up for months now, but it was just not high enough on the To-Do list on a ranch. She could do it, and get exercise at the same time with all the moving things around and carting trash out and sweeping the floor. Sure, he'd warned her to leave the garage to him. Well, he'd threatened her with a spanking if she went anywhere near it, moved one thing. And they had already butted heads when she'd gotten crazy with the chocolate sugar high and gone through closets in the house like a maniac. But everything there was so much better now.

She'd make things better in the garage, too.

Stepping further inside, she remembered the last time she'd decided to work in the garage. Dropping the can of paint, she'd been using to paint one of the walls with, onto his four hundred dollar set of golf clubs had been an accident. Who knew that pouring on a can of turpentine in an attempt to clean up the mess on the clubs would make it even worse? Sheesh! Her husband had some "choice" words to say about all of that! Then he'd found a new use for the dumb paint stirring stick. On her bottom. Just because she'd called him a first class jerk for losing his temper.

"Shoot! Shoot! Shoot!" Brandi bit out several hours later when she backed into Colby's new do-everything-but-build-a-house-itself table saw and it tipped over. She stared in horrified disbelief as it hit the cement and an ominous crack filled the air. "Darn! Darn! Darn!" He was not going to be happy about this accident.

Her gaze shifted to the small mountain of mixed screws, bolts, nails, washers, and whatever else had once been in lid-less containers on the shelf she'd knocked over earlier. A mountain of stuff she would sort out later, after she figured out how to re-hang the shelf.

Then her gaze shifted to the long scratch on the side of her nearly new Mustang from when she'd moved the wire tomato cages out of her way. And why were they in here anyway? She'd been doing so well sliding them through the narrow space, until she'd butted into a rake hanging on the wall and jerked in alarm. He was not going to be happy about that either, even if it was her car.

She wished she'd never decided to start this project. She needed to figure out if she could race into town and somehow find a new saw before Colby got home.

Startling her, her cell phone rang.

Immediately she jammed her fingers into her tight jeans' pocket to pull the phone out. It got caught on a loose thread and the ringing continued several more times before she managed, grumbling under her breath, to pull it free. Then the phone slipped from her fingers and joined the broken saw on the garage floor with another ominous cracking sound. She knew before she even picked it up that it was broken.

Could the day get any worse? It had started out so well.

Of course it could get worse. Colby pulled his pickup into the driveway at that very second. She was caught with her thumb in the proverbial forbidden pie, caught in his sacred territory standing amongst the ruins.

He did not look happy.

She tried a smile. "Thought I'd…" What could she say? She was in the wrong place, at the wrong time.

"Destroy my garage," Colby finished for her, focusing on the chaos scattered at his wife's feet. Memories of the last time she'd "attempted" to help him with the garage cleanup work flashed in his mind. Unpleasant memories.

Brandi tipped her chin up. "I was trying to help."

He ground his teeth as he climbed out of the truck and headed in her direction. "I didn't need your help in here," he said, trying to stay calm.

"I'll make things right."

He sucked in a deep, cleansing breath, released it and shook his head in dismay. "You're deadly in the garage." Then he moved toe-to-toe with her. "I believe we've discussed this matter before, haven't we? How you're not supposed to do anything in here but drive your car in and out. In and out, that's all."

Her gaze darted to her cherry red Mustang and his gut clenched. What else had she done? He swept a glance over what he could see. Nothing. It looked fine. But a glance back at his wife, with an uneasy expression in her eyes, told him different. Although he dreaded doing so, he walked to the other side of the car.

"Brandi Lynn! How the hell did you manage that scratch?" He moved until he could rub a finger along the almost two-foot long scratch. When she didn't answer right away, he decided he'd rather not know what happened. "Never mind."

"I'll get some of that bottled paint touch up stuff," she offered.

"It'd take a damn can of paint." He shook his head again and strode back to her. Frustration and resignation warred within him. He knew what must be done. They both knew what must be done, what she expected to be done. "If you don't want a spanking out here in the garage, I'd suggest you march yourself into the house."

Her hands flew back to protect her bottom. "Colby..."

"You're not talking your way out of this." He turned her toward the house and urged her forward with a firm swat. "You were warned, with good reason, about not coming out here to do anything."

"Accidents. Then and now," she protested, dancing forward as he planted another swat on her bottom.

"True enough and you won't be spanked because of accidents. You'll get spanked because you disobeyed me." He gave her two more swats before she could get through the doorway into the house. "I told you not to touch anything in my garage, and you promised you wouldn't. I don't mess with your kitchen; you're not to mess with my garage."

She gave him a challenging look. "I wouldn't care if you 'messed' with the kitchen."

He followed right behind her, nudging her toward the kitchen table and a chair. "But I care if you mess with my garage." He thought about the many other things she could have done today. "Why didn't you work on that financial statement you said you'd been struggling with? Or pay some ranch bills. You could have done a hell of a lot of other things."

She heaved a disgruntled sigh. "I wasn't in the mood for any of that stuff." It was frustrating to be back here in the kitchen, at the table where, only hours ago, he'd done something far different with her than prepare for a spanking.

"You should have been." He pulled out the chair, sat down and patted his thigh. "Now you'll be sitting at your desk with a sore bottom."

"Couldn't you just let me clean up the mess in the garage? That'll be punishment enough."

He cringed at the very idea of her going back into the garage. He couldn't afford to replace or repair any more things. "I'll clean up the mess. When I get home tonight. Right now, darlin', I've got a bottom to spank."

Brandi inched toward him; her bottom tingled already. "I'm really sorry. I guess I'm just a jinx in the garage." She stopped beside him, waiting. She'd gone against him, again. No matter how she tried, she struggled with that stupid "obey" part of her vows. Would they be doing this the rest of their marriage? Or would he get tired of having to do this someday and just give up on her? Would he decide he needed a more mature, more responsible wife? Now she was depressed.

Pulling her back from her musings, he reached out and unzipped her jeans, then shoved them down to her knees. She felt miserable standing there, but he took her hand and guided her over his lap. As she braced her hands on the floor, he gave her bottom a pair of sizzling swats.

"It's been a while since I've spanked this sweet little butt." His hand smoothed over her buttocks.

"Not long enough," she grumbled, disgusted with herself for letting her boredom lead her into trouble.

He spanked her again, twice. "Guess there's limits on how long you can stay out of mischief."

"Guess so." She stared at the tile floor thinking it was time to mop it again.

He tugged down her panties to mid-thigh. A rain of biting smacks landed all over her poor bottom. "Being 'good' for very long isn't something you do well."

"But I'm trying." She wriggled and he tucked her close. "I'm trying," she repeated.

"Well, you need to try a hell of a lot harder to listen to me, to obey me." He laid his hand down on her smarting bottom. "Your little act of misbehavior cost me dearly this time. You broke my table saw." He swatted her once. "You broke some shelves and created a huge mess." Another single swat. "And you did some serious scratch damage to your car." Another single swat.

She hated it when he listed off what she'd done wrong. "I'm aware of the damage I caused," she said on a sniffle. "I promise I won't even go in the garage again. You can even drive my car out for me."

He blew out a ragged breath, calming down. "Six more and we're done."

True to his word, he smacked and counted each of the six spanks. They were lighter, but she would still be squirming in discomfort for a little while. But she'd expected worse. Even the paddle.

Finally he helped her up, watching while she winced and pulled her panties and jeans into place. When she looked at him again, love sparked in his eyes even though his expression remained stern. "Now, march yourself into your office and get to work on what you should have been doing."

She dashed at a tear on her cheek. She didn't want to go sit and work on accounting, but it wouldn't be smart to tell him that. "I'm sorry we had to end the day this way."

"Sweetheart, I'm hoping to end the day in a whole lot more pleasant way." He gave her a crooked smile filled with promise of rumpled sheets and some serious making up.

Her mood improved. So what if she'd been spanked? She'd deserved it. But now the evening looked much, much better. "I'll even let you have your wicked way with me again, cowboy."

His eyes darkened. "I've been toying with trying out a new position, something I read about somewhere." He grinned in devilment. "You feeling limber?"

Chapter Five
Needing Her Cowboy

Brandi had acted like a crazy person all week at her office in town and at the ranch. The final tax deadline for individuals for the year was fast approaching, only another three weeks to go. She'd been bombarded with new clients running late for meeting that October fifteenth panic time. While her business focused on doing the accounting work for small businesses, she'd worked for a general tax accounting firm while in college and could handle work for individuals.

Somehow word of all that had leaked into the area's communities. No doubt her husband and his connections had talked about her. He was proud of her skills and tended to brag about her. She'd wanted to keep her client list small enough that she wouldn't get overwhelmed. But, in the last month alone, she'd gained a half dozen new ranchers and small businesses in Hinkley as clients. Enough clients that she'd needed to expand her working schedule from thirty hours to forty each week. She liked being successful, but she regretted having to spend so much time away from the ranch and Colby. She missed getting up to fix breakfast for her husband and then going back to bed until nine or ten o'clock.

She heaved a sigh, leaned over her desk and buried her face in her hands. If one more potential new client walked in the door, she would run screaming from the building. She was just one person. She could only do so much. Handling pressure wasn't something she was good at, which was why she'd decided to have her own business. Not that there were other accounting firms in town that she could have gone to work for. She was pretty much the only multi-service accountant in the county.

She glanced at her coffee cup. Empty. Again. Just like the pot in her office's tiny storage room. She needed caffeine. She needed an elf or some other magical person with amazing accounting and tax skills to come in during the night and whip out a dozen tax returns. And she needed—really needed—sex. Which meant she prayed Colby got home today from the trip he'd taken to a cattleman's convention in Dallas.

His photo on the corner of her disastrous desktop caught her attention. Lord, he was a good-looking man. Tall and muscled from ranch work. His face always needed shaving, and the stubble felt rough sometimes when he kissed her, but she didn't mind that. His lady killer eyes spoke of all the wondrous things he could do to a woman.

Although illogical, it was as if he'd deserted her this last week. He knew she wasn't good at handling stress, especially this snowballing kind of pressure. People depended on her. They needed these tax returns and they expected them to be done right. Of course, she could do that. It was just there were so many returns to do. If Colby were here to support her, to calm her down, to hug her and take her mind off all she had to get done in the next few weeks, she could handle it all.

Damn it! He shouldn't have gone off and abandoned her. Just an hour of mind-blowing sex and her world would be all right again.

She glared at the phone. They'd talked each night and discussed how things were going. He'd been happy with some new things he'd learned at the convention. He'd gone on and on about the newest in breeding techniques and the latest information on castration. As thrilling as that no doubt was to a rancher, she'd been a bit Well, yuck! about it, although she hadn't told him that.

To be fair, he'd also listened to her complaining about how one of her newest clients hadn't filed a tax return in ten years. She'd gone off on Colby about having to dig through a dozen boxes of almost all useless receipts in order to reconstruct those prior ten years so she could do the returns. He'd commiserated with her when she'd bemoaned all the paper cuts she'd gotten this week, and the ruined fingernails. But those phone conversations weren't enough for her. She wanted him back here and he'd caught the resentment for him being gone in their call last night. He had been less than pleased.

Shifting on her chair, she knew he would be dealing with her foolish resentment and unfortunate cursing at him for having decided to stay an extra day. He'd also warned he might have to give her a settling down lesson before she went off the deep end. No, she suspected, she might end up sleeping on her stomach tonight. As strange as it was, she accepted that she needed his help. Sometimes his hard hand landing on her bottom did make her feel better…not right at that moment, but later.

She glanced at the photo again and sighed. Their bed had felt enormous and so lonely this week. She'd missed snuggling up to his big, warm body. She even missed the insane way he got up so early, and she had to drag herself out of bed to make him the same boring breakfast every morning. And she missed those morning goodbye kisses that lit a fire in her all day. The goodnight kisses were pretty darn good, too. Particularly when combined with a sheet-blazing round of cowboy-does-his-wife-good sex.

She squirmed in her chair again, experienced the heat low in her body and the way her clit tingled. Darn, darn, darn! She needed him right this minute. He was never, ever going away again without her! She couldn't stand this kind of deprivation, this kind of withdrawal. It had her thinking wilder, hotter thoughts with each passing day. She'd even broken down and taken care of her desperate need on her own last night after they'd talked. It had been okay, but not the same as having Colby's nice long, thick cock inside her.

Suddenly she realized she'd been sitting here complaining to herself for quite a while. What time was it anyway? She shifted her gaze to the wall clock. Oh damn! She should have been on the road to Kansas City at least fifteen minutes ago, more like a half hour. Sitting here pouting when she should have been in her car was going to make her husband even unhappier with her. And he'd know that's just what she'd been doing. He always knew.

Snagging her purse, Brandi zipped out of the building. Maybe if she kept a good eye out for patrol cars, she could push the pedal to the metal a bit more than allowed.

***

Colby changed positions as he leaned against the building outside of the American Airlines exit. He'd been standing here, shifting around, growing more impatient and more worried with each passing minute, for an hour and a half. At least the weather was nice and cool. Not cool enough to settle him down, though. Where was she? Had something happened on the drive here from the ranch? He didn't want to even think about an accident, but he did. His gut churned.

He shifted again, started to reach for his cell phone to try and call her once more. But the calls hadn't gone through the other dozen or so times he'd tried calling her. He had a feeling she'd either lost her phone or left it at the office or at home. She had a habit of doing that lately, a bad habit.

He pulled out his cell phone anyway. He'd phone the ranch and see if any kind of emergency calls had come there. His stomach knotted again. Damn. All he wanted was to see her, hug her to within a breath of her life. Beyond his concern for her, though, he wondered if she'd still be mad at him about staying the extra day. Pouting and avoiding coming to get him. He sure didn't want to learn she'd been in an accident, but otherwise she'd better have a good excuse for being this late.

Just as he started to punch the ranch's number, he spotted her cherry red Mustang almost speeding into the curve leading toward his terminal. No accident. Good.

Relieved but irritated, he straightened and picked up his duffel bag. She pulled up to the curb, flashing him a wary smile as he yanked open the rear door to toss his bag inside. He saw the fleeting guilty look in her eyes and made a quick decision. He needed something to do with his hands or else he'd drag her over his knee for a well-deserved spanking right now, no matter who was around.

"I'm driving." He walked around to the driver's door and pulled it open. "Don't push me about this, Brandi Lynn."

Wisely, she climbed out and hurried around to the passenger's side. She avoided his eyes as she said, "I'm glad you're back."

In spite of the anger simmering inside him, he leaned over and kissed her. It wasn't a mere brush of lips either. He kissed her with the relief that she was okay. He kissed her with all the pent up desire he'd been dealing with this last week. A mere kiss wasn't going to take care of all his needs, but this was a start. But he knew there would be some unpleasant matters to deal with before they got down to the more fun parts of being married.

"I called your cell phone when I got in and got your voicemail," he said, easing out into the airport traffic. "I've been calling your phone every fifteen minutes since then. Those calls didn't even go to voicemail."

Brandi stared out the side window. "I forgot my phone at the office. Sorry. The battery probably died, since I don't have a charger there."

He was silent as he searched for the highway entrance. He was tired, had a headache, and knew he needed to catch up with Thad about ranch matters. This extra delay didn't sit well with him. "We talked about my arrival time just this morning. You told me you didn't have any meetings scheduled today and that it would be no problem. So, did something come up?"

"Uh… no. I was thinking about other things and didn't watch the clock." She glanced at him, must have seen the annoyance in his eyes, and turned back to the window.

"Other things like pouting because I went to this convention, when you wanted me to stay home with you? Or pouting because I stayed an extra day?" It still irked him that she'd cussed at him last night about his decision. He knew all the extra workload she was handling right now had ratcheted up her stress level. And he knew she was horny, which he liked. Nevertheless she needed some help with settling down. He also felt a little guilty about not being here to do it before now. It was his job to take care of his wife—in all ways. He'd accepted that when he'd said his wedding vows three months ago.

She blew out a frustrated breath. "Both, okay! My being crazy like this is your fault, you know."

His hands fisted on the steering wheel. "And why is that?"

Now she faced him, irritation sparking in her sky blue eyes. "Because I depend on you."

"I know. Including taking charge of you when you go a little nuts."

Again, guilt weighed on him. He'd let her down. She was ten years younger than him, still struggling to adjust to being a responsible adult. She'd had too many years being a spoiled rancher's daughter and pretty much doing as she pleased.

"Yes!" She raised her stubborn chin. "I know what needs to be done, what I deserve. It won't be pleasant, but you'd damn well better do your take charge thing tonight."

He raised an eyebrow. "Probably much sooner than tonight from the way you're talking."

Some of the sass went out of her, yet she still demanded, "My bottom better be good and red and sore by bedtime."

Amusement had his lips twitching. His little wife sure could be a spitfire. "Count on it, sweetheart."

***

An hour and a half hour later when Colby drove into the garage, he faced Brandi. She saw regret in his chocolate brown eyes and that his jaw was set in determination. Her stomach clenched. This wasn't going to be good. What had she been thinking, sassing at him? She wanted his undivided attention, but not in that way.

"I'm sorry for snapping at you earlier. That doesn't change anything, does it?" She couldn't believe she'd pretty much demanded he spank her. Just one more bit of proof how much she needed him in her life. But when she acted up like this, she wondered how much longer he would put up with a sometimes-childish wife like her. He deserved far better than her.

"I love you, Colby. Please don't give up on me," she said, desperation in her tone.

His brow furrowed and worry entered his eyes. "I love you, too."

But he hadn't commented on the other part of what she'd said. Heart heavy, she put her hand on the door handle. "I know you've got ranch things to do. Thad is no doubt waiting to talk to you."

"I've got a wife to deal with as well." He climbed out and grabbed his bag from the back seat. He opened the door to the kitchen and motioned her inside. Then he set his bag just inside the room. "I've missed you, sweetheart. A big old hotel room bed feels mighty lonely."

She blinked back tears, grateful for the words. Yet she knew things still weren't right between them. Not after the way she'd acted, what she'd said to him the night before. If she could take it all back…. But she couldn't.

"Get the brush out, Brandi Lynn, and be waiting for me in our room when I get back from talking to Thad."

She sucked in a breath and her body tightened with dread. Her eyes misted again, but she wouldn't plead with him to change his mind.

Before she could move, he pulled her to him. She felt the tension in his much larger body, sensed he was fighting with his decision to punish her. To let him know how much she cared about him, no matter what he intended to do to her, she swept her arms around him and pressed into him. She disappointed him time and again and she hated herself for doing so. She was trying to mature, not be so irresponsible, so needy. But it was a struggle.

He held her close and she heard his powerful heart beating beneath her ear. His arousal was evident as his hard erection pressed against her. He fingered her short hair, which she'd finally had returned to blonde as he'd requested. He'd been upset with her when she'd cut off the long length of it and had it dyed auburn right before their wedding. Her changing the color back was one of her efforts to please him.

"Have I said how much I like seeing your blonde hair again?" he asked, proving that she had pleased him. "And it's growing, too, which I also like."

"It was a bad decision, I admit it." She savored the way his fingers continued playing with her hair. His thick, dark hair was getting a little scruffy and she couldn't wait to sink her fingers into it as well. Later. When things were right between them once more.

He eased her back, studied her for a second, and lowered his head. She rose on her toes and met him halfway for the kiss. One she needed so bad. The way he kissed her long and hard told her he'd needed this as much as she had.

With a sigh, he pulled her arms away and stepped back. He hesitated and then said, "I've got to go, but I regret it." He strode back through the garage and out toward the heart of the ranch.

She closed the garage door and picked up his duffel bag. Hugging it to her, she inhaled his scent. He was finally home. Her world would be alright now. Okay, her world was going to be filled with a bit of pain for a while, but she'd get over that. All that mattered was Colby was home!

She carried his bag to their bedroom, wishing she hadn't acted so childish. She knew being upset with him for going away on business was selfish, just as he'd said. Spending so much time moaning and groaning about his being gone had wasted a lot of work time. Pouting about all of it.... Well, that was immature and not worthy of the adult she wanted to be.

Setting his duffel down, she went to his nightstand and opened the top drawer, where he kept the implements he occasionally used on her poor bottom. The well-worn leather strop her father had given to Colby not long after their marriage. The paddle Colby had found somewhere. A tube of Ben-Gay he sometimes applied after a spanking to make the sting last a little longer. Nasty stuff! And the big, wooden hairbrush he'd insisted she buy one day when they were out shopping together. He liked it, how easy it was to use, how it got her attention. She hated it.

She didn't want to even touch the awful brush, but knew he would be annoyed if it wasn't on the bed waiting for him. She should have married a man not interested in domestic discipline. She should have....

What was she thinking? Even if her husband burned her bottom now and then, she loved him with her whole heart. And she'd agreed to this occasional discipline. She could have said no and he would have accepted her decision. They had discussed all of this during their engagement.

Resigned to standing behind her decision and to what was to come, she snatched the evil brush from the drawer and tossed it to the bed. It had no sooner landed there than she heard Colby's familiar boot steps coming down the hallway. Already? No! Not yet.

He strode into the room as she moved away from his nightstand and closed the drawer. His gaze went from her to the bed. "Good girl."

"I thought you would be a while," she muttered. "I can wait...." Her buttocks were already clenching and unclenching in anticipation.

He shook his head, went to sit on the edge of the bed. "No sense putting this off. We'll get this little chore taken care of and then I'll go catch up with Thad." He patted his lap. "Come stretch over, sweetheart."

Don't do it. Don't do it. Don't do it. But her mind told her feet to move. She was so not going to like this, but she knew without a doubt her husband loved her. He might make her uncomfortable for a few hours, but he'd never really hurt her.

She stopped a few feet away. He hadn't asked her to bare her bottom and would just fold her denim skirt over her back, then pull down her panties. She decided to show him her acceptance even more and removed both her skirt and the panties. Then she pulled off her blouse as well, leaving her lacy bra on.

When she glanced at him, his eyes had darkened. His breathing appeared deep and ragged. He seemed transfixed at the sight of her and that made everything easier for her. She slid in silence across his lap, the rough denim rubbing her bare skin, making her shiver. He still hadn't said anything, so she stretched her arms out, then her legs on the mattress.

He smoothed a hand slowly over the entire surface of her bottom. It was the first halfway intimate touch from him she'd had in a week. Heat spread through her, settling in her woman's place that ached for him. His touch turned more intense, kneading first one cheek and then the other. She moaned in pleasure.

"Damn, but I've missed you, sweetheart," he admitted, his deep voice husky. "I'm tempted to forget this spanking."

"Your choice, but we both know I've earned it," she said, knowing it was the truth.

His erection pressed next to her side jerked and he caressed her bottom again. "That you have. Still...." He couldn't seem to stop smoothing his rough hand over her sensitized flesh. "I've been thinking about this spanking ever since you ragged at me, since you cursed at me."

"I shouldn't have said any of what I did. I've just missed you so much," she explained, glancing back at him. "I depend on you more than I should, I suppose."

His nostrils flared and their gazes locked as he lifted his hand and brought it down on the center of her buttocks. Not too hard, but enough to have her hissing.

He kept his hand in place, studied her, and his chest pulled in air on a deep breath. "You deserve to be spanked."

She didn't deny it, but kept her focus on his eyes, even though her neck was beginning to hurt at the strain of looking backward. "Whatever you say, my husband."

"Obedience," he said, one side of his mouth lifting in his crooked smile. "You've struggled with that ever since before the wedding. Actually, on the wedding day." His fingers kneaded her bottom right where he'd spanked her.

Longing tore through her as she felt his touch and drew in the clear scent of his arousal. The punishment spanking had turned into foreplay. "You took care of me then. You always take care of whatever need I have."

"I always will, sweetheart." He tried to look stern, but failed. "How about I paint this pretty ass a bit red? Just a bit."

The thing she'd learned about her husband was that while he didn't like punishing her, he liked having her over his knee at times. He liked the sight of her bare butt all vulnerable and waiting for his attention. And he got aroused at the hint of red on her bottom. Maybe that was odd, but she didn't really mind. Especially because he later did some very, very nice things to her.

"Maybe pink," she suggested, smiling before lowering her head to the mattress.

"Hot pink," he offered a compromise. His cock pressed against her again, enthusiastic for something else.

"I'm not even going to list all the reasons this is necessary." Then he surprised her by picking up the brush. As she sucked in a breath, he sent down two sizzling swats.

"Aaaahhhhhh," she moaned, gripping the quilt in front of her with both hands in preparation for more.

He tossed the brush away and bent over to kiss her stinging bottom.

"Hot pink, very nice."

She didn't move, confused. "That's it?"

"You want more?" he asked on a chuckle.

Since he wasn't holding her in place, she wriggled off his lap. She reached back to rub at the already disappearing sting. "So, we're good now?"

His eyes held such need, such intense desire that her heart raced. She glanced lower, at where his jeans were pushed out in front. "Want to...?"

"Oh, yes, ma'am, I do," he said with heat in his voice, but shook his head. "You know how I feel about making love right after spanking you."

She blinked at him. "But that wasn't a real spanking." Disappointment spread through her.

"I'm considering it one. Unless you are begging me for more."

"No, I'm good."

He stood but continued looking at her with such yearning.

Feeling daring and confident, Brandi reached for his belt to undo his buckle. He didn't stop her. "How about I make you feel a whole lot better for now?"

"You don't need to...." Again, he didn't move as she unzipped his jeans and then shoved them and his undershorts down to mid-thigh.

She went to her knees in front of him, wincing at the fleeting pain in her bottom. She reached for the long length of him. Holding the pulsing, hot shaft in her hands, she smiled up at him. "It's a shame this sweet thing can't do what he wants to do...what I really want it to do. You're sure?" She gave him another chance.

"As much as I want to ram deep inside you, sweetheart, I can't." His eyes were filled with regret and determination.

"Fine. Later." She leaned forward to lick the head, to swirl her tongue around it.

He jerked and sucked in a breath. "Damn! That feels good."

Pleased, she licked up and down the side of his shaft like it was an ice cream cone. He had stiffened.

"Better breathe, cowboy." She cupped his balls with one hand and stroked his cock with the other.

"You're killing me," he groaned.

She put her mouth over him, suckled him as he rocked back and forth, trembling with need.

He shoved his hands into her hair and held her to him. He'd been in control, but she was now. It was a heady feeling and she loved it.

She worked him at her own pace, tortured him. Until he'd had all he could take and gritted out, "Inside you. I need to be inside you."

She released him, grinning. "Changed your mind, huh?"

"Now. Right damn now."

Without hesitation, she stepped around him to bend over the bed. He was behind her in a flash, nudging her legs apart. Then he drove into her already wet and ready body. Two thrusts and he shot his release deep into her. With the last thrust she, too, exploded.

He sank onto her back with a relieved shudder. "Sorry, sweetheart. I couldn't help myself. I missed you too much."

Brandi laid beneath him, his half-limp cock still inside her. "I'm okay with it. I'm yours, cowboy, to spank when necessary." She pushed her bottom against him, squeezed her inner muscles around him. "To love any darn minute of the day or night."

Colby chuckled and moved against her as well. "Give me a few more minutes and I'll love you again. Properly. To hell with waiting until tonight. That is, if you're willing."

She squeezed him again, telling him just how willing she was without words. Evidently his talk with Thad could wait. She was fine with that.

Chapter Six
Naughty in Vegas

Brandi's nose was all but glued to the window of the cab. Excitement thrummed through her. It always did when she came to Las Vegas and this time was no different. Even at two o'clock in the morning the strip was alive with people and heavy with traffic. So different from back home in Hinkley, Kansas.

All too soon for her, they pulled up in front of the Stratosphere near the far end of the strip. Colby climbed out and reached in to help her, but she was already shoving open the other backseat door. She left him to pay the driver and gather their bags. From the constantly opening door leading to the casino and check-in, the sounds of slot machines being worked and loud bells going off to announce some big win lured her inside. She wanted to play. Now. She'd been looking forward to this trip ever since he had mentioned it. This was his special gift to her for surviving the October fifteenth deadline, ending tax season for the year. She didn't want to waste a minute of her time here.

She stopped just inside the doorway and looked around with all the delight of a small child at Christmas time. She had trouble containing her excitement. The flashing lights over the winning slot machines tempted her. Across the room were the roulette wheel tables with crowds gathered around them laughing and talking and urging the current player on. Nearby were the craps tables. Maybe this time she'd study the game a little more.

"Sweetheart, we need to check in," Colby said, walking up next to her and pulling two pieces of rolling luggage. He forced her to take her bag. "Come on. I'm tired and ready to drop."

Disappointment dampened down her excitement. "But…."

That don't-push-me-on-this look crept over his face. He did look tired, now that she paid attention. He'd worked hard the last few days to make sure things back at the ranch would go smooth without him. She needed to calm down.

She mustered up a smile and nodded to where she'd spotted the front desk. "Sorry, I got distracted for a minute. You know, the bright lights and all. The slots."

He gave her a tolerant look and led the way toward the roped-off area with lines of people waiting to check in from other red-eye flights. When they got closer, he said, "Tomorrow will be soon enough to check it all out."

This was the tomorrow he meant but had forgotten for the moment. It was hard, but she could be patient a while longer. She took the handle of his bag. "I'll stay here with these and you go check us in, okay?"

"You're not going to abandon the bags and disappear into the casino, are you?" Amusement danced in his tired eyes.

"I'll be good. Promise."

His gaze turned serious. "For the whole weekend. We already talked about this. Right?"

There was good and then there was pretty good, in her opinion. He wouldn't understand the difference. She'd promised not to do anything stupid, like forcing them to take out a second mortgage or anything. That was good. Pretty good meant she would edge right up to the spending limit he'd given her. Maybe go a tad over because his idea of a spending limit and hers were a ways apart. Besides, she had money of her own from an inheritance.

When she hadn't answered him, he tipped up her chin so she looked straight at him. "Right? You're going to behave this weekend, not make me regret this trip."

"Of course. I can't believe you're doubting me." She had her toes crossed in her shoes since she couldn't cross her fingers without him seeing that. She nodded toward the slowly moving line. "Go on, check us in."

He looked worried, but gave her a quick kiss and joined the line of people.

She licked her lips, tasted the trace of mint he'd left behind from the gum he'd been chewing. She heard his deep rumble of a laugh and watched him tousle a toddler's hair as the young boy hopped beside him, evading capture by his anxious-looking mother. He scooped the boy up as if he weighed nothing and handed him to his mother. She gave him a tired smile and thanked him before turning her attention back to her son. Colby was good with kids, good with most people. Someday she'd like to give him children. Not for a couple of years, though.

They'd only been married four months and she wanted more "just them" time, selfish as that may be. This trip had been a surprise for her, what he'd referred to as a reward for her not going off the deep end before tax season ended. That was appreciated, but she saw it as a second honeymoon. Not that she hadn't loved almost every minute of their first one in Cozumel.

Just looking at her sexy cowboy sent little tingles of anticipation zipping through her. She loved him so much for his patience with her, for the way he could dazzle her with his lovemaking skills. She wanted to add something new to their relationship this weekend, surprise him. In her spare time, she'd done some reading and research online about another interest—maybe not the right term—of his, spanking. Although he mostly did it when she'd tested his patience and misbehaved in an unacceptable manner. But a few weeks ago after she'd missed him during his week-long trip to Dallas and got on his bad side with poor behavior, he'd started to spank her again. Yet it changed before he'd started. Morphed into what she'd learned was called spanking foreplay. The idea intrigued her, and she imagined he would enjoy it, too.

Her husband excelled at toasting her bottom when she got in trouble with him. But there had been a few times when he hadn't spanked her too hard. Times when she'd become turned on by the feel of his hand on her bottom. She wanted to explore that. She figured her best shot at getting him to try this was here in Las Vegas, in play town USA.

***

Unable to sleep as she'd been advised to do, Brandi opened one eye. With the heavy drapes drawn across the wall of windows, the room was nearly pitch black. And quiet; except for Colby's steady snoring. She glanced at the red numbers on the digital clock beside the bed: seven-thirty. It hadn't been quite four hours since they'd gone to bed. She'd been glancing at the clock every hour on the hour. She just couldn't sleep with thinking about everything she wanted to see, to do, and to experience while they were here.

Colby had no problems with sleeping. He'd dropped off dead to the world from the second he hit the mattress.

She eased onto her back and looked at him, wondering how he could sleep that soundly. They were in Vegas! The city of extravagant hotel casinos, outrageous shows, thousands of slot machines, and shopping. Oh so much wonderful shopping possibility! She couldn't wait to hit the shops up and down the strip.

Then a memory of what had happened after the last time she'd splurged when shopping flicked through her mind. He'd gone with her to the mall in Topeka, but left her to shop for clothes for their honeymoon on her own. He'd parked himself on one of the benches with other husbands waiting for their wives to return. When she'd returned to him carrying four heavily loaded bags, he'd gotten that we-talked-about-this look and marched her out of the mall. He hadn't said a word until they were halfway home. He'd pulled to the side of the country road. Then he'd given her a lecture on wasteful spending, disagreed with her about how buying things for the honeymoon was different. He'd given her a choice: take at least half of the clothes back or get spanked for pure stubbornness. What choice had she really had? This had been about her honeymoon. She'd taken the spanking.

Okay, she had more than enough clothes already. Maybe she'd do more window-shopping than actual buying this time.

It wasn't that he was a miser or a scrooge. And they weren't poor, plus she'd made a lot more money this tax season than she'd thought she would. He might grouch a bit, but he'd let her spend a fair chunk of her extra earnings. It was just that they'd agreed to keep pretty close to a budget and save up for a cruise next year. She'd been stunned when he'd mentioned it. It was hard to imagine her cowboy taking her on a cruise, considering what a land lover he was. Still, he'd mentioned it and she planned to hold him to it. So she needed to watch her spending habits.

He mumbled something in his sleep, something that sounded much like "Behave, sweetheart." How often had she heard him say that? A lot. Good thing she loved him.

He shifted and the sheet slipped lower. As always, he slept naked. She was treated to the sight of his bare chest, the spattering of hairs that v-shaped down to tease at the fold of the sheet. Her heart fluttered as it often did when she looked at him. How had she managed to get this handsome hunk to fall in love with her? There were so many other women who would have made him a better match. But this cowboy was hers. As long as she didn't screw things up. She still worried about the high divorce rate, how different they were, how much more mature he was being ten years older than her. She wouldn't give up without a fight, though.

Ignoring his mandate about sleeping late, she wriggled her way next to him. He mumbled again. A protest? She took it as an invitation instead, flinging the sheet away, and then snuggling skin to skin, sliding her left leg over his legs. She bent her knee and slowly moved her leg up and down, her knee teasing against the part of him that immediately grew firm.

Pleased with herself, she sighed and nestled closer as her hand reached over his warm body and her fingers feathered through his chest hairs.

"Sweetheart," she heard him moan, sounding sleepy. "What're you up to?"

"Nothing. You go right on sleeping." She leaned over to kiss his chest, inhaled his scent. In truth, she wanted him awake and ready for action.

Colby snared her hand as she began trailing it lower down his body toward intriguing territory. She had a feeling he'd awakened the second she'd turned in his direction. But he'd decided to see what she would do. They'd both been so busy. It had been too long since either of them had been in the mood to play. She'd known they needed this short getaway from their responsibilities. And she thought again about her plan to test out that foreplay thing. Later. Not now.

She tugged her hand free with ease and resumed her exploration. She found the nest of hair around his hardening shaft and wove her fingers there for a second, stopping them just before touching his cock.

This time his big body tightened and he became fully alert. He clamped down on her wrist to pull her hand away. "Brandi Lynn," he croaked, "What the hell are you doing?"

She pushed up on one elbow and smiled. "Do I need to explain?"

"You're up to mischief." His eyes had darkened and his breaths came faster now. He tugged her over on top of him and his hand cupped her bottom. "Didn't I tell you to behave?"

"Behaving is over-rated." She straddled her legs over his, moved until his thick rod was sandwiched between them. It pulsed, making her ache with desire.

"My sweet brat." He swatted her bottom, which only served to excite her even more. "If I let you have your wicked way with me, will you let me sleep a little longer?"

She sat up, shifted back onto his thighs so she could stroke his cock, delighted that he was ready for this. "I'm going to ride you good, cowboy. Think you can handle that?"

His big hands reached up to mold over her breasts. As he squeezed them, her nipples hardened beneath his palms. They ached, as did every other inch of her. "So good," she purred, pressing her breasts at him in encouragement.

He flashed his crooked grin and his gaze held such warmth. "I've been neglecting you, haven't I? God, I'm sorry, Brandi."

He leaned up to take one nipple into his hot mouth. He suckled for a few seconds, swirling his tongue around the hard tip, and then lightly bit it. She gasped, squeezing her eyes shut in pleasure. When he shifted to pay equal attention to her other breast, she moaned, looked at him in adoration. He was the best lover she'd ever had, would ever want.

While he paid homage to her breasts, she stroked his long, engorged cock. The veins bulged along the side, heat radiated off the length. In reaction, moisture pooled between her legs and all she could think about was need. She lifted up and he guided himself into her body.

As she took every delicious inch of him, so many sensations tore at her. The feeling of fullness. Wicked delight at being on top. Power from being in control. She savored it all as she rose up and slid down again until his balls slapped against her bottom.

She looked down at his strained expression and squeezed him with her inner muscles. She held him tight but he moved just a little. Oh God! The tiniest movement had her trembling all over.

While she tried to stay still, he massaged her breasts. They felt swollen from his touch. Her nipples ached at being so hard. He teased them, brushed his thumbs over the nubs. She wanted him to suckle them again, but he seemed content just to knead her breasts, just to flick the nipples.

If he wouldn't give her more, she would take her pleasure another way. "Time to start my ride, cowboy," she gritted out, lifting up and almost off him. When he reached to pull her down, she drove him deep inside again. "Soooo good. So very, very good." She stayed there low on his lap and circled around on the shaft impaling her.

"Ohhhh." His hips bucked up and he went even deeper. "Dammmmmm, sweetheart."

Spurred into action, Brandi went about enjoying the ride of her life. She lifted and pistoned down hard. She squeezed him, held him with fierce control. She circled her hips and drove them both wild. She couldn't stay still. Neither could he. In seconds, she was breathing hard, sweating, moaning, working him until she arched backward and cried out, "Yeeee-haaa!"

Even as she relished the wild moment, his hands gripped her hips. He forced her up and down a few more times until he shot inside her, crying out, "Brandi! Oh, damn, Brandi!" It seemed like he kept on shooting inside her forever. They weren't taking precautions anymore, though she still wasn't real sure she was ready to have a baby. More time alone with him would be great. But if she became pregnant, she would deal with it.

She sat up and grinned down at him. "You okay, cowboy? You look a bit tuckered out."

His chest was still moving hard as he tried to catch his breath. He reached up to lightly pinch a nipple. "Quite a ride, cowgirl."

Now that her body was satisfied, excitement about being in Las Vegas fired through her once more. She shifted off him, scooted off the bed, and dashed into the bathroom. As she cleaned up and sped back into the room, she tossed him a washrag for his own cleanup.

"I'm going to take a quick shower and then go down and hit the penny slots."

Colby had barely caught his second wind, still surprised by what had happened. It had been a while since his hot little wife had gotten aggressive like that. He sure as hell liked it when she did. But he was still worn out from the last few days of getting ready for this trip. Now that she'd drained him—pleasantly drained him—he wanted nothing more than another few hours' sleep. But he worried about her going downstairs alone. She had that crazy gleam in her eye. Even playing the penny slots she could lose a lot of money. He wanted her to have fun, but he wanted her to take it slow.

He flicked on the lamp on the nightstand. "You need to come back to bed. It's still too early."

"I want to go down to the casino," she protested. "I've been waiting hours now. I don't want to wait any longer. Besides, casinos never close."

He knew that was true, but he'd rather she waited to go down there with him. "You've got all weekend to play the slots, to see things, and to shop." Plus she looked damn hot standing there all naked and flushed from their lovemaking. He'd like her back in bed, tucked up nice and close. If she'd give him a bit longer, he might even find the energy to....

She huffed in annoyance and stopped his train of thought. "Don't even go there. You need more rest," she gave him a sassy grin. "Considering what I have in mind for later."

"Later?" Hell, he liked the sound of that. Particularly the unspoken promise of something that might try his sexual stamina. "I'm all for some hot and nasty later."

She rolled her eyes, giggled. "Hot and nasty? Aren't you the naughty one, cowboy?"

He grinned and patted the bed next to him. "Come back here and let me show you just how naughty this old cowboy can be." He winked. "We can still do whatever you have in mind later."

"Focus on the later and get a whole lot more rest. You'll need it." She walked into the bathroom. "I've got what's left of today and tomorrow until five o'clock, when we fly back," she said through the open door. "I can sleep on the plane home."

Truth was he would probably make a bad showing right now if he attempted another round of sex. Still, there was something about her eagerness to hit the slots that worried him. "Maybe I should warm your sweet butt." He shifted to sit on the side of the bed. "Kind of a warning thing. A preventive spanking to remind you to be on your best behavior."

She glanced in annoyance at him from the doorway. "I've been warned and I've promised to watch how much I gamble. I will."

He lay back down, hoping he wasn't making a bad decision. Maybe he should tough it up and go down to the casino with her. He couldn't do that, though. They were still working on the whole trust issue, had been since she'd lied to him about something her friend Sarah had done. "Okay, no spanking, and, sweetheart, I'm trusting you."

"I won't let you down."

Before she turned away, she gave him one of those sexy little looks she gave him every once in a while. There was something on his wife's mind. Something naughty maybe. Something he just might like. Time would tell. For now, he needed more sleep or he'd never survive his time in Vegas with her.

***

Brandi had wandered around most of the 80,000 square foot casino in the Stratosphere, finally finding the spot in which she wanted to settle.

Sitting down on the chair in front of the Texas Tea slot machine, she dug a twenty-dollar bill out of her small purse and fed the machine. This was one of her favorites. She sat there betting the maximum over and over waiting for her chance to play the bonus round and choose derricks to release oil and points. So close, so many times. But she never reached the magical moment of making the big win.

She reached into her purse for another twenty, and then discovered she'd already gone through a hundred dollars on this one machine. Her stomach knotted when she glanced at her watch. Not quite an hour and she'd already wasted a hundred dollars. Colby would not be happy with her. Still, he hadn't come downstairs to find her yet. She had time to kill before any of the shops opened.

Planning to find an ATM, she stood and stretched side-to-side. She'd been sitting in one place too long.

Another hour later she'd lost another hundred and fifty dollars on the Wizard of Oz machine she hadn't ever played before and found fascinating. The ATM was calling her again. She had been pulling money out of a small account of her own, which was fast dwindling now. So the money she'd been losing wouldn't affect him, but she did feel a bit guilty for not planning to tell him about the losses.

She'd just started to head back to the nearest ATM when Colby found her and stopped in front of her. "How much have you lost?"

"Maybe I won," she protested, avoiding meeting his eyes.

He tipped up her chin so she had to look at him. "How much?"

Her face burned. "A hundred dollars."

"Brandi Lynn," he said her name in a way that told her he didn't believe her and wanted the truth.

She jerked her chin free and stuck it out in defense. "Okay, two hundred and fifty dollars. But it's from the little account of my own."

His big right hand clenched and unclenched, as did her buttocks. His expression warned her if they weren't standing in the middle of the casino with a number of people around them that hand would have been connecting with her bottom.

Instead he took hold of her arm and began leading her through the casino. She dug in her heels. "I don't want to go back to the room." She hissed at him.

His jaw was tight, but he said, "We're headed outside. We'll catch a cab and go to the other end of the strip."

She sighed in relief and let him continue leading her from the casino. "New York, New York. Can we go there first? Maybe we can find a breakfast buffet there. I'm starving."

As they stepped through the doors facing the Strip, his hand settled onto her lower back, and then shifted lower until it cupped her bottom. "You better calm down. And you need to slow down on playing the slots. Or else this hand is going to ruin your day."

She reached back to shove his hand away. "Calming down. You don't have to think about ruining anyone's day." She didn't want to think about it. No, she wanted a spanking later, but not a punishment one. No, no, no.

He blew out a breath. "I don't want to end the day that way either." He gave her a crooked grin. "Maybe you'd be up for another cowgirl ride. Or…."

If she thought about it much longer, she'd grab his arm and drag him up to their room right now. But she wasn't about to miss out on her day in Las Vegas. She headed toward the waiting cabs. "This cowgirl has a lot more planned for her cowboy. You just think about that for a while."

***

By late afternoon Colby was dead on his feet. They'd gone to the opposite end of the Strip and slowly walked their way back toward the Stratosphere. They must have hit every fancy mall, gone into almost every shop along the way. He'd been patient and let his wife try on outfit after outfit, even bought her a sexy little black dress. 'Course his whole plan with the dress was to have her put it on in private, and then he'd take his time stripping it off her. He was thinking about that right now instead of focusing on how sore his feet were in the boots he'd worn. Huge mistake. But boots were pretty much all he owned.

Brandi, the woman of endless energy, all but skipped down the sidewalk at his side. She stopped to smile up at him. "Thank you so much for the dress." She nodded to the numerous bags he carried like a pack mule. "And for everything else. For the whole wonderful day."

"You're welcome, sweetheart." It still amazed him how much money he'd let her spend today. She'd been so excited about getting to shop, about him going with her without complaining. Seeing her happy had made him happy. It was like that saying: Happy wife, happy life. "I like to spoil you every once in a while. Today was that kind of day."

"I was good today, wasn't I?" she pressed him with a grin and an ornery look in her eyes.

"You got off to a rocky start, but, yes, pretty good." He wanted to pull her to him and kiss her senseless, but the bags were in his way.

She grinned even more and took one of the bags. She pulled up something red, something sheer. "Since you were so nice to me today, I'm going to give you a special treat tonight."

"You don't want to go to a show somewhere?" He sure as hell didn't. He wanted to find the black dress and....

A second red thing caught his attention. Red denim? What the hell? His mouth watered with lusty interest.

"Nope. I'm more in the mood for some private fun. Some driving my man wild time." She shoved the red teasers back into the bag. "If you're interested, that is."

She was damn lucky he hadn't given in to his strong urge to take her right here on the sidewalk. He nudged her into motion. "Don't suppose we could run through the casino? Race up to the room?"

Brandi speed walked, focused on her plans for her husband. Still, it took them twenty minutes to get to their room. While he followed her inside and locked the door, she flicked on the TV. She turned up the sound to absorb any playtime noise before she raced into the bathroom with her special bag. The one from a shop she'd gone into while Colby had taken a few minutes alone to call the ranch and check in with Thad. She'd only shown him part of what she'd bought. The other item was her real surprise.

She set the bag on the countertop, her plans swirling through her mind. She was taking a chance on this but she was pretty sure that, given the opportunity, Colby would play along quite well. She sorted through the items in the bag and smiled when her fingertips touched the soft fur. Shivers went through her and warmth built between her legs, excitement, need. She'd read about this online and had been dying to try it ever since.

Colby heard his wife moving around in the bathroom, heard her pulling something from the crinkly bag. Wanting to be ready for anything and everything she might have in mind, he stripped off his clothes. He stood waiting in the middle of the small sitting room. His rod was long, stiff, and prime for seeking a special warm place. What the heck was taking her so long?

He'd barely finished the thought when the bathroom door opened and she ambled toward him wearing a red denim skirt so short he almost saw her private place, the place where his cock wanted to be. That bit of sheer red fabric he'd seen had been a bra. Well, almost a bra. More like tiny bits of silk that struggled to contain her breasts. Pebbled nipples poked at the fabric and made his mouth water. And there was a red-fringed denim vest fluttering around the bra that held his attention. She wore his black Stetson to top the hot cowgirl outfit off. Damn, she looked good.

"Howdy, cowboy," she purred, in her best Western drawl. "Ready for playtime?"

His palms were sweating. His heart thudding. His legs were shaky and his cock stuck out like a flagpole. He couldn't seem to form a verbal answer, so he nodded with a hard swallow. They needed to come to Las Vegas more often. She seemed to have a real wild side here.

"I've been kind of naughty today. Not real naughty. Just a bit." She smiled with a hint of teasing in her eyes. "Maybe you need to turn me over your knee."

He frowned. She didn't want a spanking, did she? All he wanted was sex…and more sex.

"I don't…." He began and stopped when she pulled something from behind her back. His mouth fell open. A paddle! A black wooden-handled paddle with one side of the spanking end covered with black fur. He'd never seen anything like it. Odd, but it intrigued him.

He hadn't moved an inch. Well, maybe his cock had grown another inch or two, if that were possible. She walked straight to him, took his hand, and led him to the bed. With a gentle shove, she pushed him down. He didn't resist, ready for whatever game she had in mind.

She did a slow turn in front of him, then bent so he could see that she was bare beneath the skirt just as he'd suspected. She faced him again and gave him a sassy smile. "Ready to spank my bottom with this nice little paddle?"

She planted his hat on his head and then handed him the furry paddle. It felt like the wooden one at home, except for the funny black fur. He thumbed the fur. Soft. Interesting. He thought about Brandi, about her creamy bottom. About spanking her with this crazy thing. Hmmm, sounded interesting.

Brandi's stomach had fluttered with nerves ever since she walked out of the bathroom. After his initial look of confusion, heat had entered his beautiful brown eyes. Curiosity gleamed in their depths. She wanted to skip around in happiness.

He held the paddle, studying it before he looked up at her. "Generally when I spank you, it won't be for fun. You understand, right?"

She nodded, hoping he wasn't going to back out now.

Instead he grinned. "Okay, I'm game."

She got nervous. Would there really be enjoyment for her in this gentler, sensual spanking? Or would she only be able to remember the pain she suffered during other spankings? Was this whole idea another of her stupid ones?

Colby caught her gaze and understanding filled his expression. He motioned her to him. "Trust me. I'll make it good for you."

There was that trust thing again. In the past she'd let him down, had damaged his trust in her. She was determined to fix the problem. But this wasn't about that. This was about having fun with her husband, showing him how much she loved him.

He patted his muscled thigh, his naked thigh. "Right here, sweetheart. I want your butt perched right here."

Naked. Her gorgeous husband was naked and she hadn't even noticed until now. She really was an idiot. He'd been hoping for sex when she came out of the bathroom. Well, he would get it, but first they were going to try this little scenario. And she didn't want it to go on too long because she wanted hot and heavy sex, too. Soon. Real soon.

Colby took hold of her arm and tugged her over his lap with gentleness. She decided to try out her part, since he was playing along now. "I don't want a spanking." Had she sounded bratty enough? Too meek? Too whiny?

For a second he didn't respond, and then he pushed her short skirt up higher. He smoothed his hand over her quivering bottom. "You should have thought about that before you acted so naughty," he said, making it clear that he was playing his role. He held the furry paddle against her buttocks. "You're getting a spanking with this paddle."

The softness of the fur sent shivers tearing through her. "Ohhh, that feels so strange." She sighed and arched her bottom up.

He smoothed the paddle around her cheeks. First the furry side, then the leather side, then back to the furry side. "Interesting that this paddle has two different surfaces. Bet there's two different sensations, too."

She couldn't lie still, squirmed, tempted. Did she want him to try both sides? Maybe.

The paddle lifted and he surprised her by bringing the leather side down in a sharp thwack! An instant later he paddled her again with the other side. Swoof!

She moaned. The slight sting had gotten her attention. The soft blow had intensified her feelings. Her heart raced and she smiled. Definitely interesting.

Drawing him further into the game, she gushed, "Please don't paddle me. I've been good. I'll be even better."

He swatted her again, twice with the leather side. Once with the fur side. "You know I don't stop spanking until I decide you've had enough."

He established a routine: two with the leather, one with the fur side. Repetition after repetition. She accepted the sting and the soft pats. Both had her sucking in short breaths of pleasure. Both had her pushing her bottom back to take whatever he gave her.

Her moans of pleasure got louder and she was glad she'd turned the TV on. She wriggled all over his lap, brushed against his hard cock pressing into her side. He was enjoying this almost as much as she was.

He played the game, going back and forth with both sides of the paddle, until she started feeling a steady sting from the swats with the leather side. Until she was begging for him to stop. Not from the pain, but from the need firing inside her.

After one final swat with the furry side, he said in a husky voice, "Time to take you good, sweetheart."

He forced her to stand and she did so in excitement. She trembled all over. He could do whatever he wanted. She was more than ready.

"I'm going to drive into you, fast, hard. Are you ready for that?"

His promise made her heart race faster. "Yes," she said on a gasp of desperation.

He stood and then he bent her over the bed. She leaned on her forearms, her forehead pressed against the rumpled sheets, her bare spanked bottom thrust high. He inched her legs apart and trailed a finger between them. Finding her moist, he husked out, "Naughty girl is ready for me."

"Yes, ready." She tensed as he guided his rod to her swollen lips, inched the cockhead inside her. Then he held her hips and rammed deep in one long push. "Oh, yes! God, yes!"

His answer was to pump in and out, long and deep. He grunted from his efforts. His fingers dug into her hips. "So good. So damn good."

By the time she flew apart and came in bliss back to earth, he'd reached his own climax. Her knees had grown weak and she collapsed forward onto the bed. He fell on top of her, sweating, and panting.

His hand found the furry paddle and he chuckled. "Best damn purchase you ever made, sweetheart."

She felt content and loved. "Thought you might like it."

"We're definitely taking this home with us."

So, this plan had worked. Maybe next time….

Chapter Seven
Warm All Over

"Will you pick up the book I ordered at Barnes & Noble while you're in Topeka today?" Colby asked from the bathroom where he stood shaving.

Brandi stretched like a contented cat on the king-sized bed in the adjoining bedroom. She was taking a day off from work. A much needed one. A day to do whatever she wanted, even go shopping in Topeka...as long as she paid strict attention to their budget. She wrinkled her nose at the annoying thought about anything to do with a budget. You would think being an accountant that she'd be alright with them. She was... for everyone else. After splurging on the recent trip to Las Vegas and all the shopping they'd done there, her husband was determined they get back to the budget he'd created and stick with it.

"Just for clarification, the book of yours isn't coming out of my miscellaneous spending money, right?" She understood the need for staying within their budget because they were planning to go on a romantic cruise next year for their first anniversary. She wasn't going to miss that. But watching pennies sure was a downer.

He popped his head into the doorway. "No, it's part of my money."

Lord, he was one sexy cowboy. Well-toned, every luscious inch of him in nothing but boxer shorts. She sighed and flipped onto her stomach, which made her inhale the scent of their lovemaking from minutes ago. She smiled at him. "No problem then."

His eyes darkened to molten chocolate as he took in her still naked body. She could see in his gaze that he wanted to come back to bed for another round. And then she recognized his determined resistance. Darn it. He'd already told her that he was running late and his men were waiting for him to get started on some project she'd already forgotten. Only because he'd already done all the right things this morning would she forgive him. That didn't stop her body from tingling everywhere, longing, aching.

She wiggled against the mattress and gave him an encouraging look. Would it kill him to be a little later?

To her exasperation, he didn't take her hint. And he called her stubborn.

She sighed in resignation. "You know, Best Buy is right next door to Barnes & Noble." Blast it all. She was still horny. Focus. You're not getting him back in this bed. Focus. "Do you want me to check on a replacement cell phone for you? You said yours has been acting up a lot."

"Sounds good. Nothing too fancy. No iPhone. I don't need all the extra stuff." He glanced at her. It was clear that his mind was already focused on ranch issues as he moved back into the bathroom to finish shaving.

She scrambled off the bed and headed for the dresser, found a pair of bikini panties and a bra, then tossed them on the rumpled bed. "Your money again, right?" She wanted clarification about the additional expense.

"No, take it out of the ranch's expenses." He strolled out into the bedroom and took a second to admire her as she walked toward him, then headed for the shower. He reached out and lightly swatted her bottom as she passed him more out of habit than anything else.

The soft little pat on her bare backside ratcheted up her frustrated desire another notch. Her thoughts turned to their fun little playtime in Las Vegas. That had been their first adventure into spanking foreplay with the fuzzy paddle. She adored the paddle...and the man who'd used it.

Then he ruined the memories. "You must have big plans for your spending money. Be careful, sweetheart. Remember what will happen if you go nuts with your credit card."

She stopped to shoot him a withering glance. "Yeah, yeah, I know. You'll burn my butt."

Generally when he hinted at spanking her for some breach of their agreed upon list of rules, it filled her with a sense of dread. Going over his knee with her bare bottom exposed to feel the hard slap of his hand, was not a pleasant experience. She felt ashamed at letting them both down, embarrassed. And it plain hurt. But sometimes, when she was horny—like now, the idea didn't bother her as much. He got turned on heating her bottom, seeing it turn pink, and watching her squirm. After she'd had what he decided was proper thinking time, he was all about making up. And he did that really well.

"It's such a pretty butt." He'd followed her to come back and brush his teeth.

She shivered and tried to push aside thoughts about spanking—of any kind—and about the hot making up time. "Let's not go there, okay. I'll pay strict attention to my budgeted free spending." It was hard to stay irritated at him when he looked so darn tempting.

She reached into the shower and turned the water on to heat up, wondering if she shouldn't have just left it cold. Frustration fluttering inside her, she glanced at him and their gazes met in the mirror. He'd picked up his toothbrush and started putting toothpaste on it. Still, she sucked in her stomach and hoped he didn't notice the bit of extra cushioning there since she'd stopped watching her diet quite as well. Maybe she needed to revisit doing some Pilates exercises.

"I've got plans for tonight," she said, putting as much huskiness into her tone as she could. "Something… Well, I'm not going to tell you. You'll just have to wait and see."

Now she had his attention, more so since she'd given him quite a surprise on their Las Vegas trip. His eyes widened with interest. He stepped closer, stopping inches away, still holding the toothbrush. "You're a naughty woman. Teasing me this way." He ran a hand down her arm, started to reach for a breast.

Pulse pounding and excitement tearing through her, she shifted away so he couldn't quite touch her. Pay back for not coming back to bed when she wanted him to stay for round two. She was suffering a bit, too, but it was worth it seeing his immediate frown. "Yes, but you love me."

"Damn right I do." His gaze shifted down to the hard ridge beneath his shorts. "Look what you've done, devil woman. I don't have the time to do anything about it."

"Sad for you." She giggled at his problem and stuck an arm into the shower to test the water, wiggling her bottom at him. "You'd better take some extra vitamins with you as you leave, because you're going to need the energy later."

He growled low in his voice, which did some amazing things to her body. Heat, shivers, heart palpitations.

"You'd best get in that shower before I...."

Giggling again, she stepped into the shower stall and closed the door, heard his heavy breath as he turned away. Yes, pay back was very good sometimes. She hoped he had a hard-on for hours.

"Don't forget my book." The angst of unsatisfied need echoed in his voice. "And the phone."

She stepped under the rain of warm water. Jeez, she'd already forgotten about the errands. But she would never admit that to him. Her thoughts had been focused on the fun she wanted to have tonight, and on the sale at her favorite mall in Topeka. "First thing, honey, I'll go to those places first."

"Good." He was moving away from the door when he added, "We sure wouldn't want to spend precious time tonight discussing some violation of our rules."

Irritating man. "Don't worry about me." She reached to turn the temperature up a bit more. "Worry about keeping up with me tonight."

***

Colby's footsteps were heavy when he walked into the house a little after six o'clock. It had been a hell of a long day. 'Course it was made longer by the teaser his wife had given him that morning. He'd had a hard time thinking about anything but what she had planned for tonight. She knew how to push his buttons. He still spent a lot of time remembering the hot little cowgirl outfit she'd surprised him with in Las Vegas. And the fur-covered paddle. Naughty, naughty woman. His woman.

He hung his hat on the peg by the back door, drew in a whiff of lasagna cooking in the oven and his stomach rumbled in anticipation. He was a meat and potatoes man, but Brandi's lasagna was damn good. His gaze shifted to the table by the window set with their best china and crystal wine glasses. Silver candlesticks and long white tapers had center stage. No doubt there was a salad and his favorite dressing in the refrigerator, along with their favorite brand of wine. The stereo in the living room filled the house with country music. His wife had gone to a lot of trouble.

He squeezed his hands into tight fists. She was also in a lot of trouble. If only she didn't have this bad habit of being so lead footed on the accelerator.

At that moment Brandi scurried into the kitchen, blinking in surprise at finding him there. She had on a pair of her tightest jeans. They hugged her curves in all the right ways. His thoughts were waylaid for a second, lust threatening to make him forget his worry, his anger.

"I didn't expect you for another hour," she said, her brow furrowing as she must have noted his dark expression. "Something wrong?"

He forced his gaze up from the tight fit of those jeans. But the low-scooped neck of her T-shirt snagged his attention. His palms started sweating. His cock swelled. Somehow he found the strength to battle his urges down and focus back on the problem. "Did you behave yourself today, Brandi Lynn?"

She appeared confused and then blinked, and worried her lower lip for a second. "Oh damn!" Her cheeks grew pink.

"Someone from Barnes and Noble called me late this afternoon. They reminded me that if I don't pick up my book in another couple of days, they'll put it back in their inventory." This was an annoyance, not a huge thing in reality. Yet she'd told him she would get the book. He was more upset about the other matters.

She shifted so the center bar was between them. "I meant to go there." Her voice was a near whisper, tinged with regret.

Meant to. The words rubbed him wrong. "I reckon that also means you didn't make it to Best Buy to get me a new phone."

She studied the counter top, her cheeks turning even pinker, and he had his answer.

She didn't look at him. "I went to the mall first, planning to go to those two places on my way home. Then I went to an afternoon movie. You know how much I like movies." She glanced up and away again. "By the time the movie was over, I knew I had to hurry home so I could make this meal." Now she did meet his eyes, done babbling. "Sorry."

He drew in a steadying breath and held her gaze for several seconds. "I'm annoyed as hell you didn't do those two small errands for me after you said you would. You know how I feel about following through on your promises."

She bobbed her head. "Yes. A person's word is his or her bond." She ran a finger along the counter top and added quietly, "I get forgetful sometimes. Lose my focus. More so when it's about something not real important."

He moved to stand opposite her, his shoulders stiff. "No, these errands weren't 'real important.' But you did agree to do them. I would have done them for you."

"I know." She sounded miserable and he heard the quick sniffle, meaning she was close to tears.

His gut tightened. He didn't like making her cry or feel bad. But she'd let him down, again. Sometimes he wondered if he ever would be able to trust her. Trust in a relationship was real important to him. He wished she didn't struggle so darn hard with becoming a responsible adult. There were days when he just didn't want to have to deal with her selfish ways, more so when he was tired…like now.

He tried to tromp down on his irritation. There was an even bigger issue to face. "Look at me, Brandi."

Her head lifted and she gazed at him with worry in her eyes. She swallowed hard. "You know."

It hadn't been a question but a statement of fact. His stomach churned, remembering getting the call from his buddy at the community police station a short while ago. "Yes, I know. Gary called to tease me about my 'heavy footed wife.'"

The color drained from her face. "It wasn't much of a ticket. I wasn't going that fast," she protested. "He's such a busybody."

Colby raised an eyebrow. "A ticket is a ticket. We discussed this matter the last time you got one about two months ago. And the time before that, three or four months earlier."

She couldn't meet his eyes again. "But the other times were warnings."

"Because you somehow sweet talked your way out of getting actual tickets." He drew in a deep breath, blew it out heavily. "I hate having to pay for a speeding ticket, spending money in such a foolish way."

"I'll pay for it," she offered, sounding dejected.

Patience, he had to call on his limited patience. "That isn't the point and you know it."

She glanced up once more and her eyes were glistening with tears. "I know."

He had to harden his heart before he reached for her and drew her into his embrace. He wanted to wipe away the tears. Hold her until he didn't feel sick about what could have happened.

Instead he said, "What bothers me—no, scares the hell out of me—is the thought of getting a call one day where someone tells me you died in a car accident. You're pushing your luck with your damn heavy foot."

She blinked rapidly, but tears streamed down her pale face anyway. "I'm so sorry," she mumbled. "So sorry, Colby."

"I don't want to live without you, sweetheart."

Brandi felt awful. She'd had a tendency to drive too fast ever since she'd gotten her driver's license at sixteen. So far she'd been very, very lucky. No accidents, not even a minor fender bender, like her friend Sarah had in her fiancé's truck a few months back. But she'd had warnings, a lot of them. Until today, when her luck had changed and the officer had written out a ticket. Then ratted her out to her husband, which was beside the point.

She hadn't seen Colby look so scared before he'd talked about his fear of hearing that she'd been killed in a car accident. The strain of controlling his anger with her was evident in the vein pulsing in his neck, in the tight way he fisted his hands, in the distress filling his eyes. He could be done with all of this stress in his life. He could give up on her, even if he claimed not to want to live without her. Was she worth all the trouble she caused him?

Her heart wrenched at the idea. She had to try harder to act more responsible. She could do it!

She didn't want to be spanked, but she'd earned it this time. Both of them had been raised in homes where your bottom paid a price when your brain made you do stupid things. This ticket incident and her vehicle carelessness qualified as stupid. They'd come to an agreement before getting married that he would discipline her when necessary. He took his role of head of their household seriously, including punishing her at times. Sometimes she didn't agree, but she loved him enough to trust him. He was not a cruel man.

The smell of spicy lasagna drifted around the kitchen. It was ready to come out of the oven, but it could wait. She couldn't swallow a bite at the moment, and she didn't think her husband could, either. Determined, she walked to the stove and turned the oven off. Everything else would be fine.

She had to clear her throat before meeting his worried eyes and saying, "Spanking time."

He glanced toward the set table. "Dinner?"

"It can wait."

His expression softened and she noted respect in his eyes now. His whole body wasn't as tense. Good. Well, not good for her, but she'd survive.

Colby was so proud of his wife that it was a wonder the snaps on his shirt didn't bust open. She was accepting responsibility for what she'd done wrong. The only spankings she ever initiated were the new kind, done in foreplay, she'd introduced into their lives in Las Vegas. But she wouldn't be getting a sensual spanking with the fuzzy paddle this time. And she knew that.

"Get me the wooden spatula." He needed to do this, but he wanted a little distance between them as well. She continued to look too damn good in those jeans, and he still remembered she had plans for them tonight. Plans he wanted to get to, but he couldn't ignore this situation. He didn't want the next call from his police friend to be…. He shoved the horror aside. "Now."

She flinched at his request, but turned to grab it from the nearby utensil holder. Her hand shook as she put it in his open palm. Then she waited, resignation in her pretty blue eyes.

He considered changing his mind. She already knew what she'd done wrong and why it worried him. She expected him to follow through. Giving her a gentle look, he nodded toward the counter. "Push those jeans and panties down. I want to see your bare ass. Then bend over."

For a second she didn't move, just stood there looking wary. Finally she did as he'd instructed. With every passing week, his once rebellious bride was growing more comfortable with the idea of obedience. She'd always had the love and honor of him worked out in her mind. Obeying someone else came a lot harder for her.

Putting her forehead to the marble top, she shoved out her bottom. "This is embarrassing, you know," she said quietly. "Having you see me like this."

"It's nothing I haven't seen before." It probably was embarrassing and that, he supposed, was part of the punishment. Having her stand in front of him with her pants at her knees, her pretty, creamy ass thrust out…. A definite thrill for him to see, he couldn't deny that. But he didn't put her in this position for his entertainment. Even if his cock had hardened since he'd been given time to stare at her submissive posture and the place he ached to drive into.

"This is different, though," she mumbled, capturing his attention again.

"Yes." He had to get a grip on his desire and his body's longing to….

"No sense in putting this off any longer."

She took hold of the far side of the counter and prepared for what was to come.

He picked up the spatula and put a hand on her lower back. "You will pay more attention when you drive. You will stay within the speed limits." He brought the implement down with sharp thwacks over and over on both cheeks, leaving behind small red squares.

She jerked beneath his hand, fighting to stay in place. "I will!"

He smacked her several more times and the sound of wood striking flesh circled the room. Her yelps of pain added to it and she danced up on her toes. "How many more?" she gasped, squirming.

A spanking with the spatula always worked faster than a hand spanking. Already there were numerous red splotches on her butt and he felt the heat rising off her hot flesh. But she wasn't at the point of acceptance of having done wrong, where she arched her back and cried out her misery. He was ready to be there so they could be finished with this.

"We'll see how you are after another six." He watched her suck in a breath and she grabbed the counter tighter. He would make these next smacks harder, memorable. One of his good friends had died driving recklessly and he had never come to terms with the loss. He'd told her about that when she'd come home with her first warning. She'd promised to never let him go through the experience again because of her.

It took a couple of minutes to paddle her the six times he had said. They hadn't been near as easy as the first swats. She'd hissed and wriggled with the first four of this round. She'd arched backward and cried out in misery with each of the last two. He was satisfied, relieved, too.

He turned to put the spatula in the sink while she remained in place recovering. He grimaced at the sight of the bright red butt and knew she would ache for a while tonight. Better that than her not coming home to him again, than his learning she'd been killed while driving in a non-responsible manner.

"You can get up now." He stayed back, although he wanted to hug her. She might not be ready for that yet.

She eased up and her jeans slid to her ankles, hobbling her. She didn't seem to care. Her hands shot back to cover her hot bottom and she turned to face him. "I'll do much better. I promise."

He figured she would give it her best effort. "Do that."

Unable to resist any longer, he went to her and thumbed away her tears. He gave her a quick kiss before he bent down to help her out of her jeans and panties, instead of making her pull them up. It would be easier on her, harder on him. He would have to watch his precious wife work around the kitchen and sit down to dinner with him while half naked.

Helping him out a little, she pulled an apron from a drawer and tied it on. She walked carefully to the stove and leaned over to remove the lasagna from the oven. His shaft seemed to triple in size as he stared at her sexy red bottom surrounded by the lacy white apron. He figured he deserved to suffer, too.

"I'll get the salad," he croaked out.

Spunky woman, she glanced at him and smiled, and he knew she was aware of his problem.

Brandi wasn't real happy with her husband, even though she'd deserved the paddling. At least he was experiencing an agony of sorts, too. She'd seen the bulge in his jeans.

Her bottom did sting something awful, but she would have to live with it. He expected them to eat together even when she got spanked. Not a pleasant event with her squirming on the chair at the table. Again, she'd survive. The sting should fade pretty well by the time the meal was finished. Disciplined or not, she had plans for tonight.

She sat the lasagna dish on the stovetop to let it cool for a few minutes. Her thoughts drifted to something far more enjoyable than grimacing in discomfort. She hadn't told Colby everything she'd done in Topeka. Before going there, she'd done a little research on the internet and found a shop that specialized in naughty items and a great deal of fun. He'd enjoyed the cowgirl thing in Vegas—okay, they both had. So he appeared to be up for that kind of pleasurable amusement. She was certainly ready for it. Of course, the night would have been better if she didn't have a sore bottom to deal with. Oh well, she wasn't backing down now.

"Are we having garlic bread, too?" he asked and pulled her back to the moment.

"It's already buttered and ready to go in the oven for a few minutes." But the oven needed to warm up again. She turned it on and went to reach down the counter for the foil-wrapped bread.

Colby moved behind her, curling an arm around her waist to pull her back against him. She sucked in a breath at the way the rough denim of his jeans rubbed her tender bottom. But she relaxed and enjoyed the feel of his impressive erection pressed close.

"I'm sure it stings a bit yet, but I just had to snuggle a minute," he said, his deep voice gruff. "Watching your sweet red ass wiggling around was just too much for me."

"You gave me a sound lesson, cowboy." She gritted her teeth and moved back against him, heard his groan. "That spatula is nasty."

He pushed her hair out of his way and kissed behind her ear. "Sweetheart, it was a lesson that had to be taught. How much longer are you going to need...?" He licked her neck with the tip of his tongue, finishing his comment that way.

She shivered from that spot all the way down to her bare toes. What the hell? So she would be a little uncomfortable because of her sore bottom. The rest of her ached even more for her husband. She nuzzled her butt against him one more time. "Think we could eat dinner later?"

"Works for me." He scooped her into his arms and carried her to the bedroom.

To encourage him to go faster, she whispered naughty things she wanted to do to him and that he could do to her in return. He all but ran up the stairs, wasn't even winded when they reached the landing.

The second they were in the bedroom she squirmed until he put her down. She forced all thoughts of her throbbing bottom aside and focused on her plan. "Strip. Now. When I come back into the room, I expect to find you naked and stretched out on the bed."

"Yes, ma'am," he answered with a crooked grin.

She went into the walk-in closet, turned on the light and shut the door. As she pulled off her cropped T-shirt and put on the costume she'd bought today, she heard him undressing, heard the shifting of the bed as he lay down. Her pulse raced in excitement. She hoped he wouldn't find this ridiculous, that he would play along. He had the last time.

With a settling breath, she opened the door.

Colby lay naked on the bed, covers tossed to the end, every inch of his body needing his wife. He had no idea what to expect, but he was up for just about anything. Would she wear the cowgirl outfit again? He damn sure liked it. He liked how she gave her all when she rode him, too. He still remembered her driving them both to the edge, then yelling "Yee haa!" Lord, she'd about done him in that night.

His cock was already standing up and impatient for attention. He slipped his hand around it, stroked it once. He heard the closet door open and froze.

Oh. My. Dear. Lord. She walked out wearing the sexiest nurse's dress he'd ever seen. Her breasts almost fell out of the low neckline. The hardened nipples were visible. A short, flippy skirt showed off her long legs. A little white cap was perched on her head. And she had a fake stethoscope around her neck. When she must have seen approval in his gaze, she did a model's spin to give him the full effect. Her skirt fluttered up, revealing her pretty red, bare bottom.

"Dammmmn," he groaned. "You're killing me."

She preened instead of showing sympathy. With a sexy walk to bring any man to his knees, she strolled next to the bed. She flashed a wicked smile as she focused on his hand still circling his dick.

"Oh dear, it looks like my patient is suffering. I guess I'll have to take care of your…needs. Your special needs." She licked her lips. "Won't I?"

Everything about her was making him crazy. The hot little dress, knowing she had a bare red ass beneath it and nothing more. The promise of something wicked in her blue gaze. And that voice. Seductive, breathless, fantasy enticing. God help him.

He was ready for her to climb over him. Ready for her to straddle his legs and impale herself on his steel-hard rod.

Instead she took off the stethoscope and put it on his nightstand. She opened the drawer and her face pinched in distaste as she looked at the implements he kept in there: the worn paddle, a wooden hairbrush, and a leather strop from her father. She pulled out the fuzzy paddle, something they both enjoyed. But she put it back and he experienced a twinge of disappointment.

Then she lifted out something he'd never seen before, something she must have hidden in there sometime today. She faced him with a tube of something in her hand. "This should help with your problem."

His heart raced when she showed him the label: Perky Penis. He swallowed hard. "What… What's that for?"

"It's a special lotion for my exceptional patient. Cherry Sucker flavor." She removed the cap and smiled. "You know how much I like cherry flavored things. How much I like to suck…."

Lord a' mighty, her husky, teasing voice made his struggle for control even harder. "Sweetheart…" Every inch of his body was on high alert.

When she licked her lips with the tip of her small tongue, he thought he just might have a heart attack.

Giving him a devilish look, she poured some of the lotion on her fingers and leaned over him. His gaze locked onto those breasts inches from his face. Her scent was driving him wild. Then she took hold of his shaft with her greased up hand. He about rocketed off the bed at the cool touch, at the way she moved her hand up and down his length.

"You're going to feel soooo much better very soon. I'm going to help release all this awful tension in your body," she purred and stroked him some more. "I'm going to make this pain you're feeling go away."

He couldn't keep from arching his body upward. Hell, he could hardly breathe. The temptress was enjoying this. He was at her mercy and trying to play along with her game. For now. He wasn't sure how much longer he could do it. He was sweating; his body was on fire. But she'd gone to so much trouble for this. He had to tough it up and give her a chance.

She moved her thumb to his sensitized cockhead and circled the very tip with torturous slowness. She continued the circling, moving lower, circling the whole head now, touching the slit at the top with her thumb.

That was it! He reached for her hand, but she batted his hand away.

"No, no, no. You mustn't stop your nurse from taking care of you." Her gaze danced with playfulness.

"You're not taking care of me," he protested, his face tightening as she began stroking his shaft again. "You're torturing me."

"Well, then," she said on a sigh, "I guess it's time for the next part of your healing process." She lowered her head and licked the side of his cock, along the bulging vein. "Oh, yum."

He fisted his hands at his sides. Let her do this! Just a while longer! Come on, you can take this!

Her mouth engulfed the top part of his cock. The warmth, the moistness, felt good. When she cupped his balls and went down on him even more, he thought he would lose his mind. He groaned, arching his hips upward.

She pulled her sweet mouth up his shaft, swirled her tongue around the head, concentrated on the slit already leaking pre-cum. Her hand began massaging his balls and she glanced up at him with pure mischief in her gaze. Then she swallowed him once more.

His hands moved to hold her head in place, desperate. "Best damn nurse ever," he gasped, struggling for air, sanity.

She got serious, showed him just how much pain and need he could take before she put him out of his misery. He tried to push her head away when he was about to explode, but she refused to move. She took every last drop of his semen before she pulled her mouth off him and sat back with a Cheshire cat grin.

"Feeling better, cowboy?" she asked in that seductive tone.

He couldn't move, had trouble thinking straight. "Well, damn."

She smiled and started taking off her nurse outfit. "For a compliment, that's pretty sad."

He watched her luscious body appear and arousal stirred again. "Give me a few minutes and I'll show you how much I appreciate your special kind of nursing."

She leaned over to reach in the nightstand drawer again, and then pulled out another tube of something. "Got you a tasty treat, too. Chocolate. Want to try it?"

He was getting harder by the second. He took the tube and grinned. "Lie back, sweetheart, time for my treat."

As she spread out before him and he saw the hint of pink from her spanking, he took a second to thank the good Lord she'd come home to him safe and sound. He didn't think he could live a day without her in it.

Chapter Eight
The Cattleman's Ball

It had been one of those cold, dreary early November days. Gloomy. Brandi was in a sour mood. She just wanted to stay home tonight, vegetate in front of the TV with a big bowl of chocolate ice cream. She wanted to take a long, hot bath, and she wanted to snuggle next to Colby. Very close, very intimately. But they were supposed to go to the Cattleman's Club annual ball tonight. She'd attended the ball in the past with her father and had enjoyed it, but tonight she wasn't in a partying mood. Maybe she had a cold coming on. Maybe she was PMSing. Whatever, she had a serious case of the blahs.

Determined to try one more time to change her husband's mind about going, she strolled to his home office, where he was working on ranch business. He shut down his computer and looked at her with tired eyes. She hoped that was a good sign for her purposes.

"Yeah, I know. It's time to start getting ready." He sat back in his chair, closed his eyes, and rolled his neck around his shoulders. He'd been sitting in here for a couple of hours bent over the desk. No doubt he was tired and stiff.

When he focused on her again, she gave him her best seductive smile, even batted her eyelashes. "How about staying in tonight instead? Crawl into bed, share a big bowl of your favorite ice cream." She licked her lips nice and slow. "Maybe have some fun with chocolate syrup. Sound interesting?"

"Damn tempting," he answered in a husky groan. His velvety brown eyes darkened and her hopes rose.

She perked up and started to turn away. "Great! I'll go get the chocolate syrup."

But he burst her bubble of anticipation. "We'll have to put the naughty idea on hold for another time, sweetheart. We need to go to the ball."

Darn it all! She faced him again with her shoulders slumped. "But chocolate…ice cream…me, naked."

Regret flitted over his handsome face, shadowed with daylong beard stubble. He rubbed a hand over his chin as he sometimes did when frustrated. "You're killing me, Brandi, but we've got to go. All of our neighbors will be there. Meaning a lot of your clients, some of the ranch's clients, too."

He shoved back his chair to stand and shook his head when she would have protested. "Not up for discussion. I gave my word that we'd be there. We're going."

When he said something in that manner, there was no changing his mind. His word was important to him. He stood behind it, while she still wanted to waffle a little sometimes when she gave hers. It was one of the issues between them that she was dealing with. In this instance, though, she knew he was right—they needed to attend the ball. Several of her clients had called yesterday to tell her they were looking forward to seeing her and Colby there.

"You're right," she admitted in reluctance. Not only were her clients excited about the ball, but also a couple of their neighbors had called this morning. Something about the calls had seemed a little odd, but she didn't know why.

While she mulled that over, Colby said, "I'm looking forward to seeing you in the new gown. Red, right? Didn't you say kind of slinky, too?" Heat warmed his eyes again as he waited for her answer.

She nodded agreement. Yes, she'd bought a new gown for tonight and it hadn't been cheap. He'd been the one to suggest she get one and he hadn't cared about how much she spent on it. At the time, she'd been more eager to go shopping than in wondering about this unusual spendthrift side of him. Now she was puzzled. She almost asked him about it, but the anticipation of seeing her all fancied up in his gaze changed her mind.

"Go on and get changed. I'll be up in a few minutes." He reached for his cell phone. "I need to check in with Thad one last time." He glanced at her before she moved. "Can you put out my suit, too?"

Even as much she liked seeing her husband all dressed up, she still had trouble working up the enthusiasm for tonight. This wasn't at all

like her. She liked parties, liked wearing new clothes. She just felt off
for whatever reason.

A half hour later Colby had talked to Thad about a problem with
one of the horses and changed into his suit. As he stood in front of
the dresser tying his tie, frustration curled through him. His wife was
trying his patience, mumbling in disgruntlement, but not quite loud
enough for him to understand her. Which he figured was for the best.
They were going tonight, had to be there. Usually she would be the
first one dressed and all but dragging him out the door. Tonight, when
it was important that she be there, she decided to get all stay-at-homey.
Just thinking about some quality time at home with his naked wife and
chocolate…. Yeah, he could imagine all sorts of things he could do with
some chocolate syrup.

He finished with the tie and frowned into the mirror. A thick erection
pressed at the front of his dress slacks. Thinking about syrup, Brandi,
and wicked ideas was pure torture. If it weren't for the surprise award she
would receive tonight, he'd forget about going. But he couldn't. Damn.

Aroused and annoyed, he glanced at the slinky red gown lying on
the bed. He had a feeling he'd be sporting a hard-on most of the night,
watching her in the dress, wanting to get her home and out of it. Focus!
Get her in that dress and get the hell to the party!

He blew out a breath. She'd been in the bathroom all this time
getting her make-up on. A woman didn't need that much make-up, she
sure didn't. She was stalling, big time, even if she'd agreed to go. It
was time to deal with this little act of rebellion. It was time to give her
some incentive to get a move on, a quick message straight to her sweet
butt. Something to make her bottom match her dress. Well, maybe not
that red, just a bit pink.

With a glance at his watch that only served to spike his blood
pressure, he knocked on the bathroom door and then opened it. Brandi
stood in a lacy bra and a matching thong in front of the vanity. Good
Lord! She took his breath away. It was all he could do not to take her
fast and furious right here, right now. Focus, focus, focus! And not on
your damn cock.

"What do you want?" She met his gaze in the mirror, looked mutinous.

That spark of defiance broke the spell over his fascination with her.
"What the hell have you been doing all this time?"

She waved a mascara wand at him. "It takes time to get beautiful."

"You were beautiful to begin with, sweetheart. You're time-wasting." He stepped straight to her. He'd had enough of this nonsense. People were expecting them at the ball. They needed to leave.

"Just a few more minutes," she said, attempting to ignore him.

Catching her off guard, he put a hand to her back and bent her over the vanity cabinet. He didn't waste another second before he landed a sharp whack on her bottom. "It's clear you need some incentive to get ready a little faster."

"Colby!" she squawked, squirming. "This isn't helping."

"You could have made the damn make-up from scratch and applied it by now." He gave her a half dozen brisk spanks. "You're done playing games with me."

She looked at him in the mirror with her stubborn chin thrust out. "Is it such a big deal if we don't go?"

Rock and a hard place, exactly where he was at the moment. She wanted a reason why it was so important to him that they attend the ball tonight, but he couldn't tell her. "It just is, okay? We're going."

"I'm not in the mood for making chit-chat or dancing or...."

"Can't you just accept I want to go tonight? That I want you there with me?" Frustration thrummed through him. Because of it and the mulish look on her face, he smacked her bottom two more times, and then felt guilty about it. "Please, sweetheart. I'll give you a night of chocolate loving another time. Promise."

Her bottom had moved back and now rubbed against the hard length he couldn't seem to calm down. The defiance disappeared from her expression, replaced by desire. She purred, "How about you give me another kind of incentive to finish getting ready?"

He held himself against her, torturing them both. His body ached to drop his pants, strip her down, and slam into her. No time for this.

He shifted away, breathing hard, grim with determination. "Like burning your sweet butt with the brush?" It was sitting on the vanity next to her folded arms.

"Not what I had in mind." She reached back to shimmy her thong down and bent over again to thrust her bottom out at him. "Come on. Just a quickie. You know you want to."

Colby groaned. "I want to, but I sure damn can't. Not now."

Irritation replaced her come-hither smile, but she didn't move.

He picked up the brush, thumbed the bristled side. He didn't intend to use it, but she was pushing his buttons real good.

Their gazes met in the mirror. Her nostrils flared and a teasing smile slipped into place. "Bet you can't stop at just one," she challenged him.

"Lord a' mighty, Brandi Lynn, you're in a weird mood tonight." He gave her a crooked grin as she continued to watch him. Then he swatted her already light pink butt. It wasn't a hard swat, but enough to sting a bit.

She sucked in a breath. All he'd done was light the fire of her obvious arousal. She wiggled her ass at him. "Sure you don't want to…."

He swatted her two more times, a bit harder, and tossed the brush on the counter. "Of course I want to, but I'm not going to!" He tried to settle his heart beat down, relax his raging erection. "If you want a real paddling later, though, I'll give you one."

"Thanks, but no thanks," she grumbled, and pulled her thong back into place as she straightened. Then she smiled at him. "Nice little burn you started. Not what I wanted it, but okay."

Regretting what couldn't happen, he glanced at his watch again. Nope, no time. "Five minutes, Brandi Lynn. Be ready in five minutes or I will burn your ass before the party."

***

All in all Brandi's mood continued to bounce all over the place as they drove to the VFW Hall in Hinkley. Colby was his usual silent self while driving. But she was okay with that. It gave her time to admire her breath-taking husband in his dark, Western-cut suit, with his freshly shaved face and those sexy lips she intended to spend time kissing later.

She turned to look out the side window at the passing landscape without seeing it. What was with her today? She'd been excited about this ball when they'd first sent in their RSVP. Tonight, though, spending the evening inside snuggling and loving had called to her more than showing off her new dress. Talking about playing around with creative uses of chocolate syrup had brought out the hot-mama side of her. And, oh yes, she was hot tonight.

They turned down Main Street and her thoughts shifted to her agreement to come tonight. She'd agreed because it seemed so important to Colby, which was strange. Any other time, he hated putting on a suit, although he didn't mind coming to a Cattleman's Club function. But when she'd gone to the bathroom to put on her make-up, her mind had wandered to more fun things they could have been doing. Then he'd barged in on her and spanked her a bit out of pure frustration with her slowness. He was right, she knew how to "push his buttons" sometimes.

She squirmed on the seat, feeling a tiny bit of sting now. Those few smacks had driven her desire for sex higher. She'd even teased him about paddling her with the brush! How nuts was that? Then he'd swatted her a few times. Not hard, only enough to stoke her fires even more. But she sure didn't want a real paddling like he'd threatened, though she doubted he meant it. She squirmed again, from the heat building inside her, not from discomfort after the almost-nothing spanking.

He pulled into the parking lot and found a space, then turned off the truck, looking relieved they'd gotten there. He climbed out and sped around to help her.

"You ready to behave yourself, sweetheart?" He gave her a crooked grin and she noted the heat lingering in his eyes. He was thinking about when they got home, really thinking about it. She could tell.

"For a while, but later...." She gave him a saucy smile. She let him help her down, making sure she brushed against him as she stood in front of him. "I'm still thinking about chocolate." She licked her lips for good measure, pleased when he groaned.

He moved away so they weren't touching. "You're an evil woman tonight."

Pleased with herself and teasing him, she started toward the Hall's front door. "Got that right, cowboy. And I'll show you later just how evil I can be."

It took him a minute to catch up with her. They stopped to leave their coats in the coat-check room and then he held onto her elbow to lead her to the already packed main room. The local favorite country band was hard at it. Loud, peppy music filled the hall. Now that she was here, she wanted to head out to the dance floor.

Before she could urge Colby there, though, her brother and father walked over to them.

"Looking good, Sis," her brother Daniel said, then nodded across the room to where his wife was visiting with a couple of women. "Almost as good as Patty."

"I thought you'd be here earlier," her father added. He raised a curious eyebrow at Colby. "Problems at the ranch?"

"My wife all of a sudden was reluctant to come tonight."

"Glad you could convince her, son. People would have been real disappointed if you two hadn't come."

Her father shifted his focus to her, frowning. He looked toward her bottom. "Hope whatever it took to convince you to come won't spoil your night."

Brandi's face heated. It annoyed her that he knew her husband sometimes spanked her. At least he hadn't come right out and asked if he'd done that.

Colby sensed her discomfort with the unspoken subject. He gave his father-in-law a disapproving look. "It didn't take much convincing. She wanted to show off this new dress of hers. And I think it's damn hot." He winked at her, adding in a husky tone, "Dammmm hot."

She preened at his compliment, feeling better already. "I'm going over to say hello to Patty and get some punch."

"Just watch it on the spiked punch," he said.

"Okay." She walked away wondering what that was about. He didn't like her to get flat-out drunk—which she didn't like either—but most of the time he didn't care if she got a little tipsy. She had a strange feeling something was going on that she didn't know about. Whatever it was must have to do with how much he wanted her to come tonight. What the heck is going on?

From his place within a small group of his ranching neighbors, Colby kept a close watch on his wife. She was back in her partying mood, thank God. She'd been wandering around the hall visiting with their neighbors, with their friends, and with her clients. That warm smile he so loved to see had returned and she flashed it at everyone. He was ready for the evening to end so she could flash her smile just for him.

She must have sensed him watching her and she met his gaze across the crowded room. With a hint of an ornery look, she finished off a cup of spiked punch and tipped the empty cup at him. That was her third cup in the last hour. She was playing with him, and starting to get a tad tipsy, too. She'd wobbled on her heels a minute ago. Good thing it was almost time for the special announcement.

"That wife of yours sure is sure looking good tonight," Henry Johnson, the president of the Cattleman's Club, said as he walked up and patted Colby on the shoulder. "Not a man here who hasn't noticed."

Colby was all too aware of that fact. Not only had she been flitting around the hall talking with people, but also she'd two-stepped and twirled with a half dozen rancher friends of his. He'd fought back the desire to take a spin with her on the dance floor, too. Except he was afraid if he touched her, he'd get all aroused again. Wrong time, wrong place.

"I've been watching them all, giving someone a warning look now and then." He wasn't jealous, just damn pleased she belonged to him. He looked at Henry. "Isn't it time for the announcement?"

The older man grinned. "So proud you're about to pop the buttons on your shirt, aren't you? Can't blame you." He nodded and walked toward the stage.

Colby sighed in relief. Ever since the officers of the local Cattleman's Club had told him about the special award at the last monthly meeting, he'd worked hard not to spill the beans about it. Then when she'd gotten in this peculiar mood and wanted to stay home tonight, he'd feared he'd have to tell her. It had been a close call.

He wove his way between couples and zeroed in on his wife where she stood near the refreshment table. Damn, she looked hot. The red gown cupped her generous breasts and skimmed like a glove over her body before flaring out at the knee. No matter how much she'd paid for the dress, it was well worth the cost. She was the prettiest woman here tonight. His woman. And he wanted her out of the dress. He wanted to smooth his hands all over the luscious body that lie beneath all the red fabric.

He walked right into a couple and excused himself, his face burning in embarrassment.

Brandi's feet hurt. It had been a long time since she'd spent so much time in stilettos. Her feet were going to complain for days. But she'd enjoyed getting to dance again. She'd hadn't missed a song, spun around the floor with most of their male friends. Colby, though, had steered clear of her and she was a little annoyed by that. She just might have to torment him a good long while later before she let him have his wicked way with her.

She was thinking about a way to torment him when she spotted him heading in her direction. Taller than most of the men, dark hair trimmed, and oh-my-god handsome. Her heart began racing as he drew closer. She caught the faint scent of the musky aftershave he favored and she drew in a deep breath. She tingled all over, warm liquid spreading inside her.

"Got a minute or two for me, sweetheart?" He stopped in front of her, gave her his sexy, crooked grin and looked down her cleavage.

"Stop it." In retaliation, she made sure he saw her gaze inching down his body, stopping in that certain spot.

He stepped closer and then froze when the music stopped. He heaved a sigh and moved next to her, looking expectant. She followed his gaze to where Henry Johnson stood at the microphone.

"Ladies and gents, I'd like your attention." He waited until the room quieted down. His wife hurried next to him carrying a plaque of some kind. "We've got something special to do tonight. Besides getting tipsy, making fools of ourselves...the usual party stuff."

He chuckled, as did a lot of the people.

"What's going on?" Brandi whispered to Colby.

"Something special, just like he said. Listen." He didn't look at her, but his chest seemed to swell with... pride? Then he did meet her eyes and it had been a long time since they had shone so bright, with more than love, with definite pride.

Beyond curious, she glanced toward the stage again.

Henry looked around the large room until his gaze landed on Colby. No, he was looking at her. Brandi's pulse sped up. She couldn't imagine why he was focusing on her.

"As you all know, Colby Pennington married himself a sweet little accountant. Heck, I doubt if there's a rancher in this room that hasn't taken their accounting business to Brandi."

Her face heated as what seemed like every head in the room turned in her direction. She liked attention sometimes, but this was too much. She inched closer to her husband.

"Hang in there, sweetheart." He squeezed her hand in reassurance.

"The lady is amazing at figuring problems out. Saved me some serious money this last year, I can tell you that." Henry nodded at her in acknowledgment.

An echo of "Me toos" drifted around the space.

"Earlier this year our treasurer of many years passed on, leaving us in something of a mess. Evidently he had a rather unique system of his own. There wasn't a one of us on the board who could figure it out."

Henry smiled at her again. "Brandi didn't have to help us. She's got plenty of accounts to handle without our problem. But she offered to help. Did it and refused to be paid for her work in straightening it all out, too. Told the board, she'd do this as her donation to the club and to the community."

Her face flamed even hotter. "Colby?" she asked, embarrassed, confused.

He squeezed her hand again.

Henry took the plaque from his wife and held it up. "The board decided we needed to do something for our Brandi, our little accounting angel. So we had a plaque made up. Community Volunteer of the Year."

He spotted the mayor in the crowd and nodded at him. "Joe Thorndale and the rest of the city leaders thought it was a good idea, too. Since she's helped them with a few accounting questions this past year as well."

He waved toward her. "Come on up here, Brandi Pennington. Come accept our token of gratitude."

Her stomach fluttered, nerves tingling. "You knew about this, didn't you?" she whispered in accusation, dreading going up to the stage.

Colby grinned. "Sure did. And I couldn't be prouder of you." He nudged her forward.

The crowd parted for her to walk through them. She collected pats on the back and "Congratulations!" as she made her way to the stage. She was pretty sure her face was as red as her dress by the time she stood next to Henry and accepted the plaque. She couldn't remember ever having made someone think this highly of her. It was humbling.

"This wasn't necessary," she said, a bit embarrassed. They waited for more and she sucked up her sudden shyness and said a bit louder, "Not necessary, but I thank you all the same. You have no idea what this means to me."

Applause exploded around the room. All she could concentrate on, though, was Colby. He stood at the back of the room, grinning his heart out. Of course, she'd make him pay for keeping this secret. She would rather have been forewarned. Still, knowing that he was proud of her meant so much to her. Maybe she was at last becoming a responsible adult. Maybe she really was becoming the wife he deserved.

It took another ten minutes for her to make her way back to him. She'd smiled so much at each offered "Thanks" and "Great job" that her face hurt. She sighed in relief when she reached him.

"You owe me for this little surprise," she said so only he would hear her, smiling. "I'm going to make you pay. Trust me."

His eyes darkened. "Later you can do with me whatever you want." He smoothed a lock of her hair behind an ear. Then his fingers caressed her cheek. "Right now we need to go somewhere private for a few minutes. There's a lounge down the hall."

She studied his smoldering gaze, trembled. "Are you sure this is a good idea? We could just go home."

He took her hand and led her to the main doorway, accepting a few more congratulatory comments as he hurried her down the hallway. "Too early for us to leave yet. But this is one of those have to moments. I have to get you alone, get my hands on you."

She wanted the same thing, but worried a little, too. Still, she followed him into the lounge and waited in anticipation as he closed and locked the door behind them.

"Unless you want the dress all wrinkled, you'd best take it off."

She swallowed hard at the huskiness in his tone, at the intensity in his gaze. She didn't move.

He undid his belt and unzipped his pants to free his long, hard shaft. "I've been watching you prance around all night long in that sexy gown. I can't take it any longer."

Her mouth watered and moisture pooled between her legs. She was speechless, simply ached and needed him to do whatever he had in mind.

He stroked his shaft. "I've got to drive this inside you. Right damn now."

Hands shaking, she removed her gown as fast as she could. She let it drop to the floor, unconcerned with whether it wrinkled or not. "I feel so naughty standing here almost undressed. Here where anyone could come in and catch us." She'd kept her bra and thong on, then decided to slide off the thong as well.

"I locked the door. And the music is so loud that nobody will hear us."

He tugged her over to one of the leather sofas, pulled her behind it. "Bend over, sweetheart. Show me your sweet spot I'm ready to explore."

She didn't hesitate, but leaned down to rest her arms on the back of the sofa. Filled with eager anticipation, she thrust her bottom out. She was so excited she couldn't stand still. "I'm ready, cowboy."

"Do you want fancy words?" He moved behind her.

"Words are over-rated. I want action."

He stroked a hand between her legs, nudged them apart further, and she moaned, "Don't tease me."

"I seem to remember you doing a lot of teasing, tempting me before we left home." He found her clit and lightly pinched it.

"Colby please!" She didn't think she could wait a second longer for him to fill her with his nice, long, thick shaft.

He chose that moment to be stubborn. Instead of filling her like she wanted, he slid a finger inside her, then two. He worked them there for a few seconds before he pulled them back out. "You're wet and ready."

She craned her head back to let him see her frustration at what wasn't news to her. "I've been ready for you since I mentioned staying home, brought up the idea of chocolate."

"And I do love chocolate," he answered on a grin. "I hope you bought a big bottle of it. For later." He put the cockhead to her swollen lips and plowed deep. "Hold still, sweetheart. This is going to be wild and fast."

She squeezed her eyes shut, fought to take breaths. So good! God, it was sooooo good!

His large hands moved up to cup her breasts. His thumbs found her nipples beneath the lace bra and flicked them as he pounded his shaft into her with such wonderful power. She was shoved repeatedly into the sofa back and it was pure bliss.

He rammed over and over, grunted, and pinched her nipples. "Teased me…all night…in this hot little dress."

"Worth the price?" she asked, struggling for air.

He moved his hands to her hips, held her in place. "Every damn penny!"

She was beyond focusing on anything but the feel of him. So very, very good. She panted, pushed desperately back at him. Squeezed her inner muscles tighter. So close…. "Ahhhhh," she gasped, holding her breath, frantic.

"Cum for me," he growled, pumping harder.

With one mighty thrust he forced her to the place where she stilled and cried out. "Oh Colby! Oh, oh, ohhhh!"

He held her tightly and pounded three more times before he stiffened. His warm cream erupted inside her as he roared out his release. He collapsed on top of her, his chest heaving from the exertion. "Thanks, sweetheart. I needed that."

He eased out of her with care and then stood. Brandi straightened and he handed her a handkerchief he'd dug out of his pocket. Her cowboy was always prepared.

She wiped away the juices, tugged on her thong. She faced him with a smile. "This was the best Cattleman's Ball ever."

Righting his clothes, he flashed her his crooked grin. "Because of the plaque?"

"Well, that was nice, too." She reached for her dress to wiggle into it. "Have to admit, I'm thinking this little private time was the best part."

Someone jiggled the doorknob and then knocked on the door. "Hey! You two all right?" her brother asked. "Dad and I were getting a little worried. He saw you guys leave the dance floor a while ago."

Colby's mouth pinched in annoyance.

Brandi shrugged and fought back a giggle at his sour expression. After all, this delicate situation was his fault. Not that she hadn't played a big part in it, and enjoyed it a lot. "We're fine. Colby just wanted to… to congratulate me in private. I'm sure you understand."

"Damn, Sis." He heaved a sigh then added, "I hope you're done celebrating. People are looking for you two." They heard him walk away, chortling.

Colby zipped his slacks. "He understood what we were doing in here just fine."

"I'm sure he did. I have a feeling Patty is going to get lucky tonight, too."

"Not something I want to think about." He pulled her close, cupped her bottom. "Am I still going to get lucky later as well? Still getting to drip some of the chocolate syrup all over my delicious wife?"

She reached down to palm his semi-hard erection. "As long as I get to return the favor, cowboy." She grinned in mischief at him. "I've got some real interesting ideas. A tad naughty. You game?"

He drew in a breath so deep she felt it and his shaft grew even more. "Think we could sneak away? I know a back way out of here."

"What about my plaque?" She didn't really care about it; certain someone would get it to her later.

One of his eyebrows rose. "Are you serious?"

Giggling, she shook her head and shoved him toward the door. "I get dibs on the chocolate first."

Chapter Nine
Gobble, Gobble…Grumble, Grumble

Brandi draped the handles of ten plastic grocery bags over her arms and then realized she couldn't close the trunk of her Mustang. She glared at the trunk lid as if it would lower on its own. It didn't, of course. Her arms felt like they were being torn from her shoulders. She didn't need this additional aggravation. Not when she was in a hurry, when she was expecting her in-laws for a big holiday meal the next day.

"Need some help?" Colby yelled from the middle of the ranch yard.

She considered yelling out "Duh!" but settled for, "As in immediately? Yes!" One of the bags started to slip off her arm. She jerked her arm upward to regain control of the problem bag and groaned. Pain shot from wrist to elbow to shoulder.

He raced to her side before she could step away from the car. He closed the trunk and grabbed half the bags from each of her arms. "You could make more than one trip."

"I don't have time for that." She edged around him and hurried to the door connecting the garage to the kitchen. Her arms hurt. Her feet hurt. And time was whizzing by. "I'm running way behind schedule."

He managed to open the door and let her go inside first. As they both set their burdens on the counter, he looked at her in confusion. "What schedule?"

She rolled her eyes at the slow-witted husband she loved so much. "Thanksgiving. Tomorrow. Gazillion things to do. I made an intricate schedule and I've already screwed it up."

"It's just a family meal." He started pulling items out of the bags and setting them down. "No big deal."

"Just a family meal?" She gaped at him. "It's the first meal I'm making for your relatives since we got married. It is a big deal. Thanksgiving dinner." She couldn't believe he didn't understand the importance from her point of view.

He set several cans of yams down, his brow furrowed in confusion. "They won't be expecting anything fancy."

She counted to ten, twenty, thirty, considered going higher. Deciding that wasn't helping, she hit him on the arm with a package of rolls. "What did your mother cook for Thanksgiving dinner?" She already knew, but she wanted to see if listing all of it would make him see why she was so distraught.

Colby gave her a look of disapproval at being hit with the rolls. He leaned a hip against the counter. " Well…turkey, of course, with stuffing. Baked yams topped with marshmallows. Only way I like those things."

He rubbed his beard-stubbled chin. "Mashed potatoes, gravy, green bean casserole, corn, too. Plus there was cranberry sauce and a couple salads."

He nodded at the package of rolls beside his elbow. "Rolls, sometimes cornbread as well." He smiled, a look of pure bliss sparkling in his warm brown eyes. "Pecan pie, pumpkin pie, and apple cobbler."

Her shoulders slumped. She had most of that on the menu, didn't she? When she'd pinned him about this a month ago, she'd written it down. She wanted this meal to be perfect, but at the moment she would be satisfied with pretty good.

His expression remained puzzled, clearly still not understanding the problem. Men! Got to love them. Sometimes, though, you wanted to shake them.

She shrugged out of her sweatshirt, laid it over the far end of the counter, and planted her hands on her hips. "Maybe you don't consider any of that fancy, but that's a hell of a lot of stuff to prepare." Especially for one meal that lasted maybe an hour, more like a half hour.

"We don't need all of what I mentioned." Yet she heard the wistfulness in his tone. He wanted all of that.

"I am not disappointing your family by serving them a half-ass Thanksgiving dinner."

She already felt unworthy of having married him. She'd seen hints of that in her mother-in-law's eyes. She was ten years younger than Colby, a whole lot less mature, even she couldn't deny that. But she was trying to become the wife he deserved, the one she wanted to be. She had a long way to go to come anywhere close to competing with her sister-in-law Sally Ann, his youngest brother Corrie's sainted wife.

"You won't disappoint anyone," Colby said, sounding patronizing.

Bopping him on the head with a can of yams seemed like a good idea. Instead, she went back to emptying the bags, tossing out a head of lettuce, stalks of celery, a bag of carrots. Had she forgotten the salad dressings? A second of panic shot through her until she breathed a sigh of relief and pulled out four different bottles of dressings from one of the bags.

When she glanced up, her husband was still standing there, looking perplexed by her obsession with emptying the bags. She did not need a distraction. "Go away. Go back to your chores and leave me be. I don't have time for chit-chat."

Stubborn man that he was, he ignored her order to leave. He turned, snagged the jug of milk, carton of eggs, tub of butter, and carried them to the refrigerator. "You're getting a bit testy, sweetheart. We talked about this just the other day. All I want is for this to be a nice holiday get-together with my family. I don't want you getting irrational because of it. I worry about you."

"I'm not irrational. I'll accept testy, but I've had a bad couple of days." She had worked out a detailed schedule of when to prepare the various menu items. Like the pies, which she'd meant to make yesterday. "Everything would be just fine, if I hadn't had that client with an accounting emergency yesterday." Now she was behind schedule and doubting if she could get back on track.

"I can help." He walked over to grab the frozen corn and green beans from where she'd set them on the counter. "Just tell me what I can do."

Stressed or not, when he gave her his crooked grin and stood there looking so damn hot, she wanted to forget everything but him. She wanted to take her handsome cowboy straight to the floor. She wanted…. "I do not have time for that," she grouched.

His thick eyebrows pinched together. "What are you talking about? I only offered to help." He studied her and then grinned in male smugness. "Oh, that." His gaze darkened, distracted from what they'd been discussing. "Maybe if we did some of that first—"

"Get your mind off your dick's needs. It's not happening. Not, not, not." She didn't need this added frustration right now. "All I want from you right now is to stay the hell out of my way. Go deal with ranch things. Let me handle the dinner preparations. Alone."

His lips pinched in annoyance. "I don't like this, Brandi Lynn. Remember what happened when we had the Fourth of July barbecue with our friends?"

She stiffened her shoulders. He would have to bring up the unfortunate incident. "I remember."

The simple answer wasn't enough. He held her gaze. "What happened that day?"

With a sigh, she admitted, "I got a little carried away with food preparations." She raised her chin. "But it was our first big party with the neighbors."

"You went crazy. You refused to let any of the others bring food, even though they all offered." He looked straight at her. "What else happened that day?"

Her buttocks clenched in memory. "I got spanked," she said in a frustrated whisper.

"You got spanked and...."

"Okay! I got paddled, too. Happy now?" She well remembered the incident, not a bit pleasant. Okay, he was right. She'd gotten out of control. She should have accepted help with the food. She wasn't Superwoman. It wasn't fun smiling and getting to know everyone better and spending the evening standing.

His expression hardened. "This is fair warning, Brandi Lynn. If you get crankier, there'll be a spanking in your near future. Understand?"

"Yes." She was done with this conversation. Just go away.

His big shoulders slumped. "I don't like talking about the possibility. But I will do it, if it's necessary. So, please, sweetheart, calm down. We can feed them peanut butter and jelly sandwiches for all I care."

Brandi sniffed back a tear of stress. "But I care. This is important, to me." She needed a hug. Just one simple hug and she could pull it together again.

As if he'd read her thoughts, Colby walked across the room and pulled her into his arms. She liked the warmth of his big body surrounding her. The familiar scent of outdoors, leather, and pure man smelled so good. She melted into him. It would be so nice to just let him take her upstairs, let him spend a few hours—or all day—taking her mind off of everything. He could do that so very well. She sighed.

He held her close, his heart thudding against her chest. When he rubbed against her and her body came alive in response, she knew it was time to stop this. She didn't have time for playing around.

She eased away and gave him a tired smile. "Thanks, I needed that."

"Me, too." He touched the side of her face with a calloused hand. "Are you going to calm down now?"

She bobbed her head. "I'll try."

He started to say something, probably another warning, but instead he accepted her word and left the house.

***

The sun had already set and things around the ranch had settled down for the day. Colby kicked off his boots in the back porch room and decided to veg out in the great room watching TV for a while. When he passed through the kitchen, Brandi was up to her elbows cooking for tomorrow. She stirred a pot of boiling cranberries and mumbled something about men at holiday time. Something about how little they did to help. Getting up as late as they pleased. Pigging out on food they didn't have to make. Parking themselves in front of the afternoon football game. It pissed him off to hear her complaints, but they were pretty much true. He figured it was wise to give her some space for a while longer.

Except watching TV bored him. Besides, he felt guilty about her sweating away in the kitchen, working far harder than she needed to for tomorrow. He understood her wanting to impress his family. He'd experienced much the same thing in the past, wanting to impress her dad. Thank God, he was past that.

Still, he didn't think his family would care what was served tomorrow. Well, sure, there were certain foods kind of expected at Thanksgiving. But they could do without them.

He was thirsty. Did he dare step foot into the kitchen again? He should check on her, try again to offer his help. She hadn't wanted it earlier, preferring to be left alone. Maybe she'd changed her mind.

He climbed off the sofa and padded in sock-covered feet toward the kitchen, cautious. As he stepped into the doorway, he watched hot juice splatter up out of the pot, hitting her forearm.

She yelped, "Damn, damn, damn!"

Colby was at her side in an instant. He turned the heat down and reached for her arm. Little red spots caught his attention. "We'd better run some cold water on that."

"It'll be fine." She jerked her arm back. "The cranberries are almost finished. The pecan pie needs to come out of the oven. I don't have time—"

He frowned and pulled her arm toward him again. She grumbled in irritation, but he looked it over with care. "The spots don't look all that bad. We can put on some salve after we deal with your immediate issues."

He picked up the oven mitts from next to the stove and nudged her to the side. "I'll get the pie out. You take care of the cranberries."

She stirred the cranberries a couple more times while he put the pie on a nearby hot pad. "There's still so much that needs to be done. Your parents, your brothers and sister-in-law are coming tomorrow. I don't know if I can do this."

"Sweetheart, I'm worried about you. None of this matters." He hated seeing the stress marring her pretty face, the exhaustion in her eyes. He should have just taken them all out to eat tomorrow, somewhere. He didn't care where. Even a fast-food place in Topeka would be okay with him.

"It does! And I wish you would stop saying it doesn't." She pulled in a breath, blew it out deeply. She attempted a weak smile. "I can handle this. I just get a little panicked now and then."

She was heading toward a full-blown panic. He needed to prevent it if he could. As she carried the pot of cranberries to another hot pad, he asked, "What else can I do to help?"

"You can put those two pumpkin pies in the oven." She nodded at two cookie sheets with pies sitting next to the stove. "After that, you can go back to watching TV. I'm fine. I'm just going to work on stuffing the turkey."

"Your arm?" He glanced in concern, but already he could see the red spots were fading.

She shook her head. "It's okay."

He put the pies in the oven, watched his wife move to work on the turkey, and walked away, not knowing what else to do. "Call me if you need me."

Brandi was relieved when he left the room. She knew he wanted to help her, but she wanted to prove to him and to his family that she was capable of doing this. He worked hard from sun up to sundown, often doing backbreaking work. She ought to be able to handle cooking a few things.

Okay, she was a little more stressed out than usual because of being behind the schedule she'd set for herself. She didn't do well under a lot of stress. But she'd get her act together.

Five minutes later, she sighed and couldn't stop staring at Big Tom on the counter. The stuffing she'd already mixed up sat in a bowl next to it. She couldn't make herself jam the bread mixture inside him. Many times in the past she'd helped her aunt with Thanksgiving dinner preparations. She'd watched the older woman do this, thinking nothing of the messy chore. But Brandi had kept her distance from touching the pale looking turkey. She shuddered and not for the first time.

Knowing she couldn't keep putting it off, she reached into the bowl and grabbed a handful of spicy cornbread stuffing. It oozed between her fingers. She grimaced. Yuck! Grimacing in distaste, she shoved the handful into the carcass. Yuck! Yuck! Yuck! Then she forced herself to repeat the task over and over. Each time, she hated the feel of the soggy stuffing squeezing between her fingers. The act of putting her arm into the dead bird's body was making her nauseous. She wasn't eating any of it!

The act of stuffing the turkey, the still stinging cranberry burns on her arm, the stress of putting together all those pies, all of it was taking its toll on her. She was failing at this task. Tears trickled down her cheeks. She blinked her burning eyes. But she had to finish this unpleasant chore. Then she needed to check her list, see what needed to be made next. She couldn't rest until…forever, it seemed.

She thought she heard footsteps in the hallway, but dismissed the notion. Her focus had to stay on this job. She jammed one last handful of stuffing inside the turkey and breathed a sigh of relief. Then she tied his flailing legs together and stepped back.

"Okay, big boy, fly yourself right into the roaster." Of course the twenty-pound turkey just sat there on the counter mocking her. Sucking up her disgust at touching the slimy turkey body, she attempted to lift it and failed. The bird slipped in her arms and almost fell to the floor. "Shit! Shit! Shit!" she yelped, juggling as best she could.

Colby seemed to appear out of nowhere, thank God. He plucked Big Tom up and planted him in the large electric roaster. Then he turned her to face him, his expression tight as he thumbed tears from her face. "As soon as you finish whatever needs doing to this turkey, you and I are going to have a little discussion."

"Discussion?" she asked, half listening.

"Not so much talking. More a discussion with my hand connecting with your bare butt."

Tears continued sliding down her cheeks and she quivered in her exhaustion, tuning him out. Her mind mulled over the menu and she tried to remember if she'd made everything in advance that she could.

"How early do I need to get up?" she asked, not expecting an answer.

"Brandi Lynn."

She blinked and came back to the moment. He studied her in clear concern. She'd spaced out on whatever he'd said. "What did you want?"

He shook his head. "You. Upstairs. Five minutes tops."

"But I need to…" She saw the grimness in his expression. "You're going to…."

"Give you a settling down spanking? Yes." He went to her and touched her cheek, wiped at the tears again. "After that I'm putting you to bed, too. Putting us both to bed." He headed out of the kitchen. "Five minutes. We've both done too much today."

Weariness weighed her down as Brandi climbed the stairs. She didn't have time to be distracted from all she still needed to get done. Going over her husband's lap for a spanking would be a definite distraction, in a number of ways. Although she didn't want a spanking, she realized that she'd needed to get out of the kitchen. It had become her prison. That was all she needed, though, just a few minutes away from her daunting tasks.

When she walked into the bedroom, she found him sitting on the side of the unmade bed wearing only his undershorts. Her breath caught. One simple look at him did that to her. He was so handsome, so sexy. And he was sitting there watching her with heated eyes. He'd pulled the covers back clearly with the intention of going to bed soon. Delightful magic happened on that bed. Her stomach felt quivery and liquid warmth started moving through her.

Until her gaze noticed the bedside clock: almost eight o'clock. Panic shoved all thoughts of enjoying her husband far away. She couldn't go to bed now. She needed to get at least one of the salads put together.

"Stop thinking about the damn meal. You've done enough for the day," his quiet tone captured her attention. "Come here."

She looked at him. His gaze held determination as well as exhaustion.

Like her, he had been up before the sun and worked hard all day long. Unlike her, he did this every day. She'd worked this hard barely a couple of days. Guilt for not being able to handle it made her feel ashamed.

"This isn't necessary," she said, "I just needed a few minutes away from the kitchen. I'm better now."

He shook his head. "You need more than a few minutes away," his voice had turned deeper, huskier. He motioned to the short, pink satin and lace nightie he'd laid on the end of the bed. "Get your nightie on, and then come to me."

She stared at what he'd chosen for her to wear. He'd gotten the nightgown for her birthday this year. What he liked best about it was taking it off of her. Maybe she didn't have to rush right back to the kitchen.

Yes she did! Still, she ached to move her hands over every inch of those work-honed pecs, thread her fingers through the spattering of chest hair.

"Brandi Lynn."

Her pulse racing, she came back from her mental wandering and walked over to pick up the nightgown with shaking hands. She drew in the scent of his arousal, which forced the heat building low in her body to burn hotter. On trembling legs, she went to change clothes in the bathroom.

It took her a couple of minutes to change and to get some control over her desire. She felt sexy and not as stressed as a few minutes ago. She doubted he intended to give her a disciplinary spanking, since they both knew she hadn't done anything wrong. He just wanted to take her mind off the craziness of cooking for his family. A warm bottom and at least some snuggling for a bit with him would settle her. He was very good at snuggling.

Moisture already beading between her legs and anticipation thrumming through her, she walked back into the bedroom. "I'm ready." As she caught his darkened gaze sweeping over her, she couldn't be more ready for him.

He focused on the nipples, which immediately pebbled. "Are you, sweetheart?" He gave her the crooked grin that made her go weak in the knees. "Come here," his deep voice echoed with desire.

She couldn't resist him if she tried, which she didn't want to. Heart pounding, she went to him. Her palms were sweating. Her lower lips pulsed with yearning. She didn't resist at all as he guided her over his lap. She slid forward into the familiar position, feeling the satiny gown beneath her stomach and the hardness of his muscled thighs. His hard shaft nudged her side making her even more aware of him, making her tremble.

"I really like this little nightie." He played with the edges of it where it stopped on the middle of her buttocks. Then he smoothed his hand over her bottom. "I like this sweet ass, too."

She quivered. In spite of the submissive position, she relished his touch and the gruff way he spoke. When he trailed a finger over the crease of her buttocks, she sucked in a breath and the shivers became more intense inside her.

He shifted the thin fabric up over her back, but he didn't lower the skimpy panties. His big hand smoothed over her bottom. She moaned, arched up into his touch. "Oh, cowboy," she said on a sigh. If he did this much longer, she would beg him for anything...do whatever he wanted.

"My little wife is struggling today, isn't she?" He gave her a light swat on one cheek. "She needs her husband to help her, doesn't she?" He swatted the other cheek just as lightly.

Brandi pushed back against his hand still lying on her bottom cheek. The swat had served to make her more sexually frustrated. "Yes... struggling, Yes, I need you," she pleaded, breathless.

His hand danced against her bottom a few times until she experienced the tiniest sting, until she couldn't lie still. "I love having this pretty butt over my knee." Smack. "I love watching it quiver beneath my hand." Smack. "Letting me do this is such a gift, sweetheart. I treasure it, as much as I do you."

She was pulling in short breaths, aching with desperate need. But she heard his words, recognized the honesty in them and his love for her. All of it meant so much. She would always be able to handle life's problems with Colby at her side. She'd gotten so lucky when he'd chosen her for his wife.

She craned her head, blew the short hair out of her eyes, and met his gaze. "Thank you."

"For what, sweetheart?" His hand smoothed over her bottom again at the same time his erection pressed closer. "I'm the one who is thanking you."

She couldn't seem to find the words to express all that she felt for him, settled on, "For being you."

He grinned, studied her for a second. "I think this distraction has helped. You don't look as panicked." He eased her legs further apart to stroke her over the moist panties, chuckling when she squirmed and gasped. "Okay, maybe you're starting to appear panicked in a whole other way."

She lowered her head, panting. "I need…I want…Ohhhhhh." His playful fingers were driving her mad.

She was about to beg him to make love to her when the oven's timer dinged loudly through the house. In that instant she drew in the smell of pumpkin pies. Darn it all.

"I need to take the pies out of the oven." She attempted to get up.

He held her in place and sent down a hard smack! "You're done for the day. I'll get the pies out."

Thoughts of the salads flashed into her mind. "But I need to make a salad." She wriggled again.

"Done for the day." He spanked her once more, but lighter. "All you need to do now is go to bed."

It was hard to let go of what she'd planned to get done. It was hard to give up this interesting experience, too. As if he sensed her troubled thoughts, he stroked a long finger between her legs, again. Her thoughts scattered.

The persistent timer blared on and on. Finally he stiffened and growled, "Damn thing!"

He set her on her feet, stood, and started out of the bedroom. "Be right back." He stopped and looked back at her. "Bed. When I come back, I expect to find you in bed. Waiting for me."

Seeing the warmth and promise in his eyes, there was nowhere else she wanted to be. With him. For a good long while.

***

Brandi felt like a new woman the next morning as she leapt out of bed with the first sound of the alarm. She hurried to grab clothes and dash toward the bathroom. Colby had just managed to turn over, his eyes still closed. She considered dropping the clothes and jumping her delicious husband, but he was worn out. He'd spent a great deal of time distracting her last night…she'd thanked him in so many inventive ways.

But the real world was back and she still had a lot yet to be done. Doubts swirled through her. How could she get everything done? Her mother-in-law was going to think she was the worst daughter-in-law ever. Maybe she should show her the plaque from the Cattleman's Club that she'd been awarded earlier this month. Would that impress her?

She dressed in record time and sped back through the bedroom. All the tension that had plagued her yesterday had returned full force. She flew down the stairs. The turkey. Was it done? Was it too done? Did she need to bake another pie? Were three enough?

The phone rang at the same time she stepped into the kitchen. A glance at the caller ID warned her it was her in-laws. Her stomach tightened. "Hello," she answered and prayed they were still several hours away.

"We should be there within the hour, Brandi," her mother-in-law said cheerfully. "We'd have been there by now, but Corrie and Sally Ann's plane was late getting into Kansas City. You remember we're all driving together from Kansas City, right?"

"Yes, Dorothy, I remember." Less than an hour! "I'm looking forward to seeing you all again." Not exactly a lie.

A scrambling noise sounded in her ear and Colby picked up on the other house line in the bedroom. "Hi, Mom. Everything okay?"

Brandi could almost hear the smile in her voice for her oldest son. "We're all so anxious to see you. See you both."

"Looking forward to it, too, Mom. Brandi's been working like a demon getting the dinner ready."

"Whatever she makes will be just fine."

Brandi pursed her mouth in annoyance. Her mother-in-law sounded like she didn't expect much from the meal and was resigned to being disappointed. Before she could say something she'd regret she disconnected on her end.

***

After enduring the longest family dinner in history, Brandi forced yet one more plate into the dishwasher and considered demanding a divorce and then moving to Alaska. She'd live the rest of her life as a hermit, maybe in an igloo. Did they have igloos in Alaska? She just wanted to be alone, to never eat turkey again, to never nibble on another piece of pumpkin pie.

Familiar boot steps interrupted the first blessed moment of silence she'd had since her in-laws arrived four hours ago. She held her breath in anticipation.

"Mom and Dad are getting ready to go into Topeka. My brothers and Sally Ann are going, too. They're getting hotel rooms there. Something about not having been invited to stay here." Colby did not sound at all happy.

"But they're coming back later, to eat leftovers, right?" She poured detergent into the dishwasher and turned it on. She was looking forward to a few free hours.

Colby walked closer and turned her to face him. "What did you say to them?"

She stiffened. "I didn't say anything. I assumed they were staying with us, assumed you asked them. They're your relatives, you know." She thought the meal had gone alright, thought she'd made some progress with her in-laws. Now this.

"Mom seems to think they're not welcome. She thinks you and I are having some problems, since you were rather tense during dinner." His eyes sparked with annoyance.

Defensive, she raised her chin. "Tense? Hmmm, let me think why that might have been. Oh, I know. Your mother doesn't like me. I'm not perfect like your sister-in-law. I can't cook like your mother, make everything just the way her precious son likes it." Tears misted her eyes. She'd tried, she really had.

His mother stepped into the doorway and Brandi was certain the older woman had heard what she'd said. Her face flamed.

To her surprise, Dorothy rushed across the kitchen to step between her and Colby. Her mother-in-law's eyes glistened with tears and she pulled Brandi into her arms. She almost hugged the breath out of her. "Oh, sweetie, I'm so sorry. I didn't mean for you to feel that way."

"Mom, she's just tired. She didn't mean what she said." Colby's glance at Brandi warned that there might be an appointment with his hand in her near future.

Dorothy looked at her son in clear disapproval. "Of course she's tired. She's been cooking for two days and trying her best to impress her mother-in-law." She set Brandi back, still holding onto her. "Until you said those things to my son, I'd forgotten all about how I once felt the same way. For years, Conrad's mother had me trembling in my shoes every time I was even near her. My husband was an only child...and talk about spoiled."

"I'm sorry." Brandi's face was so hot. "Please don't go to a hotel.

We've got plenty of room." Had she been over-reacting? She'd just been so nervous about this dinner.

"Of course they're going to stay here," Colby stated like there was no question about it, although he didn't sound as angry now.

Dorothy released Brandi and shook her head. "No, I believe you newlyweds need your privacy. And your brothers think so, too. Corrie in particular thinks so."

She winked at Brandi. "Sally Ann may have had something to do with his decision. I heard her whispering what I'm pretty sure was something suggestive in his ear. I think it had to do with needing privacy themselves that they sure wouldn't get here with so much family around. He got her a room with a big whirlpool tub." She blushed. "Well, they haven't been married long, either."

Now Colby's expression appeared uncomfortable. Too much knowledge of something personal, Brandi was sure. It made her smile.

"You and Dad, and Chad are welcome to stay here. Let Corrie and Sally Ann go to the hotel," Brandi said, offering her olive branch again.

Conrad walked into the room, focused on his wife with pure adoration in his eyes. "About ready to go, Dot? Turns out the hotel had two of those rooms with the fancy tub. I'm thinking…"

Brandi watched Colby's face burn red and he looked like he wanted to be anywhere but here hearing about the possibility of his parents sharing that kind of tub. Of course, she understood. This wasn't the kind of thing you wanted to think about your parents doing. Still, it gave her hope that Colby would be thinking such naughty thoughts for many years to come.

A now blushing Dorothy rolled her eyes at her husband. "The children, Conrad. Watch what you say."

He tossed a cocky grin at Colby and took his wife's arm to lead her away. "Save those leftovers for tomorrow, Brandi. We'll be staying in tonight. We're old, you know. Need our rest. Go to bed early."

Colby groaned and leaned against the counter, unable even to tell his family goodbye.

Brandi yelled after them, "Come anytime in the morning."

"We might sleep in a bit," Dorothy called back and giggled. "We'll be here around noon."

A couple of minutes later Brandi heard the front door close after the departing in-laws. She'd moved to the doorway to make sure they left.

She glanced across the kitchen at her mortified husband. He needed a distraction from thoughts and visions he didn't want to consider.

She tugged off the T-shirt she'd been wearing and tossed it to the floor. When her hands moved to remove her bra, his eyes widened. Exactly what she wanted. She tossed the bra down with the shirt.

"What are you doing?" he croaked, watching her unzip her jeans.

Shoving them down and then reaching for the panties, she said with wicked intent, "Getting naked, cowboy." She smiled. "I'm going to jump your bones. Unless you object."

He was already ripping at his shirt. "Hell no!"

Just to torture him, she shoved away her jeans and panties, strolled toward him, trying to look thoughtful. "I wonder how big those tubs are? Big enough for two? I'm thinking that's what…"

Colby ground his teeth a second, pressed his eyes closed. "Stop that! I do not want to think about my parents in the damn tub."

She grabbed hold of his stiff shaft the instant he'd shoved down his jeans. He sucked in a breath. "How about you deal with you concentrating on me instead?" She stroked his rod.

His face creased in frustration. "Damn! Got in such a hurry I didn't even take my boots off. Can't get my jeans off."

She went up on tiptoes and rubbed against him, lifting a leg, which he latched onto. Without even having to explain what she wanted, he helped her wrap her legs around him. She slid down onto him with ease and they both sighed. She squeezed him nice and tight. "We'll get those boots off later."

"Works for me." After that neither of them cared anything about his boots.

Chapter Ten
Christmas Crazy

Brandi sneezed and then sneezed again. No, no, no, no! This was so unfair, getting a cold just before Christmas. Her eyes burned and her throat felt scratchy. She'd gone through two boxes of tissues yesterday and must have drunk a gallon of orange juice. But she'd refused to take cold pills because they always made her sleepy and a little bit loopy.

If it wasn't the week before Christmas and she still had a million things to do, she would pull the covers over her head and sulk about being miserable. She didn't have time for that.

She flung her legs over the side of the bed as Colby walked out of the bathroom. Wearing nothing more than boxers, he made her heart do all kinds of fancy dances. What her man could do with his hands, his mouth, and most definitely with his glorious manroot! She loved the term, which she'd discovered in an historical romance she'd read yesterday.

Her pulse began racing with anticipation. Maybe she could put off some of her chores. Maybe he could as well. What would it hurt if they took the whole day off for themselves?

Before she could make the suggestion, she sneezed again. Stupid cold!

Instead of looking hot with desire for her, her husband gave her a pitying glance. "You should stay in bed today, sweetheart. Get over this cold."

No sex. He didn't have to say anything because she already knew his answer. Besides, she didn't want pity sex. If she couldn't have full-out, light the sheets on fire sex, she didn't want it. Well…there was the manroot thing….

Irritated, she heaved her body off the bed, tugged at the hem of her over-sized T-shirt, and shook her head. "Can't. I have a list as long as my arm of things to do." She held her arm up for an example, and then reached for a tissue on the nightstand.

He walked closer, but, with her stuffy nose, she couldn't even draw in his scent. After putting a palm against her forehead, he said in concern, "I don't feel a fever." He pulled her into a hug and stroked her head. "Have I mentioned how much I like your hair? Your special shade of blonde is almost completely back." He slid his fingers through the shoulder-length strands. "This is a good length, too."

She snuggled into his warmth and mumbled, "Thanks." Her moment of rebellion just before their wedding in June remained a sore subject between them. He'd loved her pale blonde hair that fell almost to her waist. She'd wanted a personal change along with altering her status from single to married. The decision to dye it auburn had been terrible, but this still wasn't her actual normal color. He didn't need to know that.

"Aren't you worried about catching my cold?" She savored his arms around her another second, and then stepped away. "You shouldn't get too close to me."

He chuckled, making his brown eyes shine with amusement. "If I was worried, I wouldn't be sharing a bed with you." He reached out to tilt up her face. "I wouldn't have made love to you last night."

He'd come upstairs to the bedroom exhausted from a hard day dealing with some runaway cattle. Yet he'd taken one look at her and gone back down to the kitchen. Her big, tough cowboy had soon returned with a bowl of microwaved chicken soup and proceeded to spoon feed it to her. She hadn't been hungry, but no way would she reject his need to take care of her. After that…oh my! The things he'd done. Far better than any of what the heroes from her beloved romances had done.

"You're blushing, sweetheart." He flashed his sexy crooked grin as if he knew what she'd been thinking. He'd teased her about what she'd been reading, asking how he compared with the men in her stories. She had only smiled at him. His ego was already big enough. He hadn't cared about her response telling her, when she screamed out his name as he brought her to a climax, he pretty much knew he met her needs.

He glanced at the erotic book on her nightstand and his grin grew bigger. "Maybe later you can share with me something new you've read about that I need to try."

"Well, there is…." She let the comment fade away and gave him a wink. Then she sneezed and ruined the moment.

He took her by the shoulders and spun her back toward the bed. "This is where you need to spend the day."

"But…"

He swatted her bottom, encouraged her to climb back between the sheets. "End of discussion."

She had no intention of lazing about in bed all day, but she wasn't up to arguing with him. So she slid back between the rumpled sheets and let him tuck her in, which was rather nice. He leaned down and she waited in anticipation for the kiss, but he kissed her forehead.

"That was sure disappointing," she grouched as he stepped away, chortling.

Her eyes drifted shut while he dressed. What would a few more minutes of sleep hurt? Somewhere in the fuzziness of near-sleep she thought he said something about her staying put today or else. Or else what? But she was too groggy to care.

***

Cookies! The word jumped into the bizarre dream she'd been having about chasing Colby around the snow-covered yard, both of them naked. She hated being pulled from the dream. Still, as reality shoved its way back into her mind, she recalled how she hadn't made even one Christmas cookie yet. And she'd promised the men that she would. She also remembered how they'd rattled off at least a dozen different kinds they favored. They worked so hard. How could she let them down? Okay, she'd get up and bake cookies, but only six kinds.

She yawned, stretched, and her shoulders ached. Her body's issues weren't going to keep her down any longer.

Half way to the bathroom she realized she hadn't even started decorating the tree Colby and Thad had hauled inside a couple of days ago. Her cold had hit hard at that point and she didn't care about much of anything. She knew Colby's parents had left boxes of decorations in the attic. He'd said something about them getting their own decorations, but she knew he'd be happier with the old familiar ones, at least this year. Maybe next year they'd look for some that would have special meaning just for them.

So that was another chore she wanted to accomplish today, too.

As she stood under the shower, letting it pound the fogginess from her brain, she recalled all the presents that needed to be wrapped. She had gifts for the ranch hands, for Thad and Sarah, for her father and his fiancée, stashed in the guest bedroom. Then there were the gifts she'd gotten for Colby hidden all over the house. He'd said they should each get just one nice present for each other. Yeah, right! It was Christmas.

She always went a little nuts with gift buying and buying for her husband was no exception. She might have gone overboard and he might decide to warm her bottom for doing so, but she didn't care. Some things were worth the price.

Colby had been concerned about Brandi ever since he'd left the house several hours ago. She could be one contrary woman at times. That cold had gotten to her, but she was close to being done with it now. Thank God. When she had any kind of health issues, he got a bit over-protective. Ever since they'd learned earlier this year that she was a borderline diabetic he'd been worried. The idea of dealing with diabetes scared him more than it did her. For the most part, she tried to eat better and stay away from sweets. But she'd had that momentary lapse of good sense when she'd run across some chocolate she'd stashed away a while back. As far as he knew, she'd resisted another sugar binge since then. He intended to keep her on the straight and narrow about that, but it was tougher during the holiday times.

He closed the door to the tack room, relieved he'd finished with the last of the repairs on a couple of bridles. There were still more chores to help with, but he couldn't shake an uneasy feeling that had swept over him a few minutes ago. His gut told him his wife was going against his warning for her to stay in bed and take another day to rest.

With a glance at his prized mare and her new foal in the nearby stall, he grinned. The foal was trying to prance around his mother on long, wobbly legs. The mare studied him in maternal tolerance. Colby did a lot of that with Brandi—patiently kept watch over her. Sometimes his task wasn't easy. Obedience was something she struggled hard with. Even on the day of their wedding she'd fought against wanting to include the word obey in the vows. In truth, he hadn't cared either way. The matter had become important to her, though, stressed her out. He'd helped her then and he would keep on helping her however necessary until he went boots-up one day.

Unable to get past the sinking sensation inside him, he left the barn and strode for the house. As he'd suspected, his stubborn wife wasn't in bed any longer. Hanging up his jacket in the mudroom and toeing off his boots, he heard the shower running.

Resigned to having a showdown with Brandi, he headed upstairs. He didn't want to warm her sweet butt, but if that's what it would take to get her to do as he said, he would. She was going to stay in bed if he had to tie her there.

"Brandi Lynn," he called out, knocking firmly on the bathroom door. "Why are you out of bed and taking a shower?"

"Because I wanted to," she grouched and turned off the water. "Aren't you supposed to be busy with chores?"

"The men will handle them until I get back." He opened the door and found her stepping out of the shower, snagging a towel, and frowning at him. His whole body went stiff. Lord a' mighty, she was a beautiful woman. He wanted to toss the towel to the floor and then….

He ignored her scowl. "You're going right back to bed." It was a statement of fact, not a question. He desperately wanted to get in bed with her, snuggle her close, and make sure she stayed there.

She dried off, seeming to take extra care, move extra slow with the task. Teasing him, taunting him because he'd invaded her space. He curled his hands into fists and tried to will his erection to calm down.

Holding his gaze, a hint of mischief in hers, she took her time wrapping the towel around her. "I don't need your help with this." Her chin tipped up. "And, no, I'm not going back to bed. I took some cold medicine and I'm much better now."

He blew out a shuddery breath as she walked by him, brushing against him in the doorway. "I came up here to spank some sense into you."

She faced him, shaking her head. "I don't think so."

He went over the list of issues that bothered him. "You're ignoring how your body still needs rest. I'd bet my best hat that you're planning to head down to the kitchen and bake those damn cookies for the men."

She didn't deny any of it. "I have a cold. I'm not on my deathbed, Colby. I'm better. Enough said."

"You're medicated," he protested. "Your eyes still look kind of watery. Your nose is red and you spent the last three days blowing it. You don't have a dime's worth of energy. You're just being plain old stubborn."

"I'm trying to get back to my life." Then she sneezed and almost dropped her towel.

His gaze shot to where her breasts pushed at the upper edge of the towel she clutched tighter. Then he shifted it to where the towel barely reached her mound. He began sweating and his cock hardened again. His body's reactions frustrated him. She was sick. They were having a minor argument. Poor timing for his desperate need for her to reveal itself.

"Which is it, cowboy? Do you want to turn me over your knee for a spanking?" She focused on the bulge in his jeans. "Or do you want to master me in bed?"

"I don't master you in bed," he countered. He did like to be in charge, but not all of the time. He'd been very appreciative that day when she'd worn the hot cowgirl outfit in Vegas and rode him until he'd nearly stroked out. And there'd been plenty of other instances she'd had her way with him.

She smiled, said in a husky tone, "Maybe those are some of the times I like best."

He blinked, swallowed hard. This wasn't going at all the way he'd planned.

"Are you trying to entice me into spanking you?" She hadn't, but that's how he wanted to see it.

"Want me to get the fuzzy paddle?" She let the towel drop to the floor.

Hell, yes! But she was trying to distract him, make him forget about his determination to get her to stay in bed. And not for sex.

Evidently she realized he wasn't interested in playing around now— he was, but wouldn't—because she huffed in annoyance. "I don't have time for arguing with you. I have things to do."

He refused to lower his gaze beyond her chin. "All of which can be handled tomorrow or the next day."

"You came out of your mother's womb stubborn, didn't you?" she accused.

He shrugged. "So I've heard."

Brandi saw in the set of Colby's jaw, in the flare of determination in his eyes that he wasn't going to be swayed on the matter. He intended to warm her bottom if she refused to go back to bed. She hadn't even succeeded in tempting him with the hint of some quick, raunchy sex. Darn, pigheaded cowboy.

As much as she didn't want to screw up more of her day, she would have to let him do this. He needed to spank her more for himself than because of her. It was no doubt another of his head of household matters. Whatever.

"Fine. Do it." She marched over to the bed and stood waiting for him, tapping her foot in impatience. "Well?"

A hint of amusement flashed in his eyes and he walked in her direction. "Determined to get your way even in this, aren't you, sweetheart?"

She didn't answer because they both knew that was her intention.

He sat down and started to reach for her arm to help her into position. She shoved his hand away and stretched over his lap, feeling the rough denim against her stomach. She moved forward until her bottom was posed just right.

He chuckled and she knew this wasn't going to be bad. He was more worried about her than angry. Plus she'd pretty much dared him to spank her.

He cupped her bare cheeks with a large hand. The calluses against her soft flesh were more enjoyable than not. When he gave a slight squeeze to her right buttock, her stomach tightened. Warmth filled her from awareness of her husband and moisture beaded on her nether lips. Did he notice?

"Ah, excited, are you?" he said, wiping at them with a finger. "Naughty woman."

"It's not too late to use the fuzzy paddle," she offered, pressing into the thick erection at her side.

Again he chuckled. "Not this time, sweetheart." His hand lifted and her buttocks tightened in expectation of the first smack. The solid crack of his hand made her suck in a sharp breath. She hadn't expected it to be so hard.

He tucked her closer and she prepared herself for whatever he had in mind. His hand lifted and returned with a much softer spank. "You're sick and it worries me."

He began a steady stream of light spanks that were to let her know his disgruntlement with her, but not any kind of anger. "This cold has been hard on you this week. On me, too."

She heard the concern in his tone, his love for her. She should have taken the cold medicine earlier on and she might not have gotten so sick. He'd tried to get her to do it, but she'd resisted. Just another incidence of her immaturity, she supposed. A small rebellion.

"I don't deserve you," she whispered in misery. "How can you keep showing me so much patience? I let you down all the time."

His hand stilled. "You can be a bit irritating at times, but, sweetheart, you don't let me down all of the time. Almost never." He helped her stand and took her hands to keep her in front of him. "We've had our issues off and on this year, like any newly married couple. But I couldn't love you more."

She sobbed and threw herself into his embrace. "Oh, Colby."

It took her a while to make up with him, to prove to him how much she loved him. When he left her in bed a good hour later, he was grinning...and very well satisfied. So was she.

***

Walking away from his naked wife had been damn hard to do. Colby adjusted his package in the too-tight jeans and headed down the stairs. He could have gone another round or two, but she really did need some rest. In truth, so did he. That cold hadn't kept her from giving as good as she got.

Once he'd satisfied himself that his men were handling the chores just fine, he drove into Hinkley. He would pick up the fencing materials Thad had ordered. And he had another errand to run.

He started up Main Street and spotted Brandi's small accounting office and pulled up out front for a minute. Small sparkling lights surrounded the big window. She'd put up a tree there, too. At least this tree was decorated. He and Thad had hauled an eight-foot tall tree home the other day, but she hadn't gotten around to decorating it yet. Her cold had hit by then. He felt guilty about the long list of holiday things she wanted to get done, which would include decorating the tree. There was no reason he couldn't help out with some of the stuff on the list. Maybe not the cookie baking, though. He could tote his folks' decorations down from the attic tonight and decorate the tree for her.

"Colby Pennington!" Annabelle Anders shouted at him and whacked his front bumper with her cane.

She hobbled with amazing speed to his side of the truck. He rolled down the side window and grinned at Hinkley's oldest living citizen. "Afternoon, Ms. Anders."

"I got that special order necklace in yesterday. Mighty pretty. Brandi's going to love it." She hobbled back around to the passenger side. "Give me a ride home and you can pick it up."

"Be glad to, ma'am." She'd had a jewelry store in town for most of his life, but closed it last year when she decided to retire at eighty-seven. But she still had connections and took care of special orders for people. He'd worried that his custom-designed necklace wouldn't make it in time for Christmas. "I'm sure glad it made it here."

She crawled up onto the high seat alone, because she frowned on anyone helping her. "I told you I'd get it."

He drove her home without getting to say another word. She was a talker and she had a lot to say about his wife. He never tired of hearing about Brandi and was damn proud of her. He didn't understand why she seemed to think she was unworthy of him, or so she'd sobbed out earlier. She'd mumbled about her being irresponsible and trying to get better. Something about him thinking she was too young for him, too. He'd done his best to quiet her tears and prove to her how much she meant to him. He thought he'd gotten through to her, but he'd also gotten lost in their lovemaking.

Turning into Annabelle's driveway, she finished up her praises. "That sweet wife of yours worked a miracle for me, I tell you. She re-worked the last three years of my tax returns, managed to get me back a bunch of my hard-earned money when I most needed it. Yes, that Brandi is brilliant. Best accountant ever. I'll be sending everyone I know to see her come the start of the next tax year. You tell her that, hear me, boy?"

"Yes, ma'am. She'll be right appreciative, too." His chest swelled with pride, he was surprised the snaps on his shirt didn't pop. His wife was a special woman, in a lot of ways.

Even though he was anxious to get home again, it took him an hour, two cups of coffee, and half a dozen cookies before he managed to walk out of Annabelle's house. Snowflakes the size of silver dollars had started falling. The clouds overhead looked thick with snow. He needed to pick up the fencing and get headed home.

He glanced back at the white-haired woman who barely came up to his shoulders. "Thanks again, Ms. Anders."

He patted the small box in his coat pocket. The whole gift-buying thing was hard. He'd suggested to Brandi that they only get each other one gift, but he knew his wife. She wouldn't have listened. She was a shopper. She loved giving gifts and he was okay with that. He was just slow witted when it came to picking out gifts himself. What if he bought the wrong size? What if it was the wrong color? Did she already have something like it and he'd forgotten? The list of his worries went on and on.

But when he'd run into Ms. Anders and she'd gotten him to talking about Brandi, she'd come up with some suggestions from the jewelry she sold. Then when he'd seen this necklace with the delicate red rose on a whisper-thin gold chain, he'd made his decision. Brandi was his precious rose. He'd never known he could be so sappy about something, but he was about this necklace. He just hoped like hell it would be enough for her. Maybe he'd take her shopping or somewhere special after the holidays. Maybe that would make up for the lack of presents from him under the tree.

He headed back to his truck when Annabelle called after him. "You give that pretty gal of yours an extra big hug for me, you hear."

"Yes, ma'am." He wanted nothing more than to get home, to crawl into bed with his wife and get skin-to-skin with her.

Brandi looked out the front window for the hundredth time, searching for signs of Colby's truck coming up the ranch road. The pretty big snowflakes had turned into a blizzard about an hour ago. He should have been home by now. Darn it anyway, he should have heard about the snowstorm headed in their direction. He shouldn't have gone into town. She was going to give him a serious piece of her mind when he got back!

Tears stung her eyes as she turned to face the tree she still needed to decorate. Stupid cold had kept her from doing so much. Well, that and she'd fallen asleep for a while after he left the room. She'd woken up to see snowflakes fluttering by the open blinds on the window. She'd wanted to put up the decorations, but she'd ended up being too worried about Colby. She'd put them up tomorrow.

She glanced at her cell phone she'd been carrying around and ground her teeth. She'd been calling him every few minutes for the last hour and just getting his voicemail. Frustrated, she started to punch in Thad's cell phone number and tell him to go track down her husband. Then she spotted headlights turning into the ranch yard and knew they belonged to Colby's truck.

Relief rolled over her. Irritation as well. He'd about worried her to death.

Impatient, she sped into the kitchen which smelled of the gingerbread cookies she'd made especially for him. She stood next to the center counter and tapped her bare foot on the tile.

He opened the door, didn't notice her and sniffed the air. "Gingerbread. You've been baking, haven't you? Dammit, Brandi Lynn."

"Even if I made them just for you?" she countered, snagging his attention.

His eyes widened at the sight of the see-thru red baby doll she'd bought for Christmas and decided to wear for him tonight. She was doped up on cold medicine and ready to enjoy her husband, again. And every hour on the hour all night. Or until he just couldn't manage anymore.

"You should be in bed." His voice was husky; his hands unsteady as he shed his coat and hat and hung them on pegs by the door. "Did you at least rest some?"

"I'm done with talking about my needing to rest. Done, done, done. Do you hear me?" A tear threatened to slip out of the corner of one eye. "I've been worried about you," she added on a sob, motioning out the window. "The weather.... What took you so long getting home? And why didn't you return my calls?"

"The road was crappy and I had to all but walk the truck home." He heaved a disgusted sigh. "My damn phone is acting up again."

His gaze was focused on her breasts, more so on the hardened nipples, as he walked closer.

"I made your favorite cookies, didn't cook any for the ranch hands. Just you." She sniffled, embarrassed about having this emotional breakdown. But she'd been terrified something had happened to him.

He touched the side of her face. "I'll brag on that to the men tomorrow."

She turned her cheek into his palm, savored his tender touch. "I bought this with you in mind." She glanced down at her nightgown. "I decided not to wait for Christmas to show you."

His eyes darkened in appreciation. "I'm glad you got impatient." He gave her the crooked grin she loved. "So, can I take it off of you now?"

Her heart raced and moisture pooled low in her quivering body. "I made a fire in the fireplace, spread out a blanket in front of it."

He got the message and his nostrils flared with interest. "Sounds good to me."

She took his hand and dragged him into the other room. When they stopped by the blanket, she looked at the bare tree waiting nearby for her attention and guilt spread through he. "I'll decorate it tomorrow. I promise."

"No," he said quietly. As she glanced at him in confusion, he added, "We'll decorate it tomorrow."

"But you've got chores to do."

He caressed her face. "I've got a wife who has been feeling bad and needs help. I can spare some time for you."

"I'm sorry I was such a problem for you today." He never ceased to amaze her.

"Sweetheart, I shouldn't have nagged at you and I apologize. I just care so damn much." He drew in a deep breath, released it and his eyes had turned to a molten dark chocolate. "How about you take the pretty little thing off? I'm afraid if I tried, I'd end up ripping it away."

Trembling from the promise in his gaze, she almost ripped the nightgown and panties off. But she wanted to wear it again for him on Christmas morning. As she set the pieces on the end table a couple of feet away, he hunkered down in front of her. His hands took hold of her hips and she shivered. Was he going to…?

He captured her gaze, his expression determined. "I've been wanting to do this ever since I first spotted you in the skimpy nightgown."

He leaned forward, his mouth moving closer, his warm breath brushing over her muff. He held her in place and his magical tongue sought her out.

She held his head to her, threaded her fingers in his scruffy hair. Heaven help her. So many sensations tore through her, the strongest being how much she cherished her cowboy. It didn't take long before he had her crying out, "Oh. My. God! Yes!" Her knees went weak and she would have collapsed if he hadn't held her.

When she'd recovered enough, he leaned back, grinning in smugness. "There's nothing like making my woman scream out."

"You can do it any time you want, cowboy," she sassed. "Any damn time."

Still grinning, he said, "I got you something special for Christmas. Just one gift, though. But I hope like hell you'll like it." His fingers were finding their way to where his tongue had been seconds ago.

She had trouble thinking straight. Yet she saw the vulnerable look in his eyes. She managed to stroke the side of his beard-roughened face and smiled with all the love she felt for him. As he'd said earlier, it hadn't been an easy first six months of marriage for either of them. And she imagined they'd continue having rough spells, but she was determined more than ever to make this work. They weren't going to be one of those divorce statistics.

"All I'll ever need is you, Colby Pennington. Anything more is just extra."

"Back at you, Brandi Lynn Pennington." His eyes looked watery, but he was back to grinning. His fingers hadn't moved, still barely inside her.

The emotion could have been expressed better, more romantically. She didn't care. This was the man she loved. She gave him a saucy look and prodded, "Back to what you were doing. Focus. On me. It's all about me now."

When his thumb flicked her clit and lightly pinched it, she moaned.

His eyes sparkled with amusement. "Yes, ma'am. It'll be my pleasure, ma'am."

The End

About the author

Starla Kaye wears many hats professionally and as a writer. She is the community coordinator for a Midwestern accounting firm, a gerontologist who volunteers with an active group of senior adults, a mentor/teacher of writing, and a multi-published author. She dabbles in writing romances of many sub-genres: contemporary, historical Western, medieval, sci-fi, fantasy, paranormal, and Regency. To date she has published 20 novels, 37 novellas, 7 anthologies, and 15 short stories.

Also by Starla Kaye

Cowboys in Charge

Seven stories of strong, loving cowboys and the women who try their patience. These are romantic stories with a touch of domestic discipline/ spanking.

Too Much Red at Christmas Time
Lizzie has a bizarre addiction to Christmas shopping and she can't help herself, even knowing she will face the wrath of her husband who believes in domestic discipline.

For the Love of His Cowgirl
Amber misses the fun little games she and Adam used to play. There never seems to be time for steamy sex, or even the spankings he'd occasionally given her for various infractions of rules or for misbehavior. Can she entice him back; get the dwindling fires of their love going again?

Cowboys and Their Toys
Jennifer loves Jason and she'd trusted him as he'd led her into the BDSM lifestyle. But now he wants to take things to a more intense level and she's balking at it. Will she lose him if she doesn't agree to go 24/7?

Plus four more equally hot stories of cowboys and the women they love.

Other titles by Starla Kaye

Our Lady Gloriana
Cowboys in Charge
Holly's Big Bad Santa

Latest titles from Black Velvet Seductions

Playing By His Rules by Glenda Horsfall
The White Spider of Savignac by V. L. Smith
Right Place, Right Time by Leslie McKelvey
Playing for Keeps by Glenda Horsfall
The Love She Wants by Mila Winters

See more of our titles at
www.blackvelvetseductions.com

Our titles are available from:
Amazon
Smashwords
LuLu
Nook
Blushing Books
All Romance eBooks
Bookstrand
and other retailers

www.ingramcontent.com/pod-product-compliance
Lightning Source LLC .
Chambersburg PA
CBHW031113260626
47172CB00001B/353